'Did you hear that.'

Alice's forehead creased. 'I'm not sure.'

She took another turning and suddenly they were back in the Main Hall again, its oversized Christmas tree looming over the staircase. From beyond the next set of doors she could hear the dying chatter of people at the fundraiser, the last few guests still hanging on in there. But that wasn't the noise that had caught Liam's attention.

The sound rang out again, and this time there was no doubt in Liam's mind about what he was hearing. He knew the sound of a baby crying well enough. From the age of ten upwards it had seemed every foster home he'd gone to had had a new baby—one he'd been expected to help look after.

'Did someone bring their baby with them tonight?'

Except he couldn't see anyone nearby, and the cry had sounded very close.

As if it was in the room with them.

'I don't think…' Alice trailed off as the baby cried again. Then she stepped closer to the tree, taking slow, cautious steps in her long, shimmering dress, as if trying not to spook a wild animal.

Liam followed, instinctively staying quiet.

The crying was constant now, and there was no denying where it was coming from.

Alice hitched up her dress and knelt down on the flagstones, reaching under the spread of the pine needles, dislodging a couple of ornaments as she did so. Then she pulled out a basket—not a bassinet or anything, Liam realised. Just a wicker basket…the sort someone might use to store magazines or whatever.

A wicker basket with a baby lying in it.

Dear Reader,

Christmas has always been a very magical time for me and my family, but I know that isn't the case for everybody. My hero and heroine in this book—Liam and Alice—certainly have little reason to celebrate the season, and no family as such to spend it with.

But we all know that life can change in an instant. One small moment, one seemingly insignificant choice, one letter from a solicitor, one job offer, or the tiniest pause between silence and a baby's cry— any one of them can alter a person's world for ever. And in this book they all do.

I wanted to give Liam and Alice a Christmas to remember—but, given their starting point, they both have to work to get it! I hope you enjoy their journey and that all your Christmases are magical.

Love and seasonal sparkles,

Sophie x

NEWBORN UNDER THE CHRISTMAS TREE

BY
SOPHIE PEMBROKE

First Published in Great Britain 2017
By Mills & Boon, an imprint of HarperCollins*Publishers*
1 London Bridge Street, London, SE1 9GF

© 2017 Sophie Pembroke

ISBN: 978-0-263-07013-2

MIX
Paper from
responsible sources
FSC **FSC C007454**

This book is produced from independently certified FSC paper
to ensure responsible forest management. For more information
visit www.harpercollins.co.uk/green.

Printed and bound in Great Britain
by CPI Group (UK) Ltd, Croydon, CR0 4YY

Sophie Pembroke has been reading and writing romance ever since she read her first Mills & Boon at university, so getting to write them for a living is a dream come true! Sophie lives in a little Hertfordshire market town in the UK, with her scientist husband and her incredibly imaginative six-year-old daughter. She writes stories about friends, family and falling in love—usually while drinking too much tea and eating homemade cakes. She also keeps a blog at sophiepembroke.com.

Books by Sophie Pembroke

Mills & Boon Romance

Wedding of the Year

Slow Dance with the Best Man
Proposal for the Wedding Planner

Summer Weddings

Falling for the Bridesmaid

The Unexpected Holiday Gift
Stranded with the Tycoon
Heiress on the Run
A Groom Worth Waiting For
His Very Convenient Bride
A Proposal Worth Millions

Visit the Author Profile page
at millsandboon.co.uk for more titles.

For Auntie Judy

CHAPTER ONE

LIAM JENKINS SQUINTED against the low winter sun as he looked up at Thornwood Castle in the distance and tried to imagine it as home.

He failed.

The dark grey of the stone walls, the rise and fall of the crenellations, the brooding shadow it set over the English countryside...none of them were exactly friendly. When he'd dared to dream about the idea of home over the years, he'd pictured himself somewhere warm and bright and welcoming. Somewhere near the beach and rolling surf of his country of birth, Australia. A house he'd designed and built himself, one that was purely his, with no bad memories attached.

Instead, he had a centuries-old British castle full of other people's history and furniture and baggage.

And it was starting to rain.

With a deep sigh, Liam leant back against his hire car and ignored the icy droplets dripping past his collar. Instead he wondered, not for the first time, what on earth his great-aunt Rose had been thinking. He hadn't seen her at all in the fifteen years before her death, and before their disastrous meeting in London he'd only ever visited Thornwood once. Two encounters in twenty-five years didn't make them family, not really. As far as he was concerned, she was just another in a long line of relatives who didn't have the time or the space in their lives or homes for him.

Even that first time he'd visited her, he'd known instantly that Thornwood Castle would never be where he belonged. Thornwood, with its buttresses and echoing stone walls, lined with rusting suits of armour, was a world away from the small home he'd lived in with his mother on the Gold Coast. Possibly a few hundred years away too. As a ten-year-old orphan, still grieving for the mother he'd thought was invincible until she wasn't, the prospect of staying at Thornwood had been terrifying. And that was before he'd even met Great-Aunt Rose in all her intimidating glory.

Thinking of it now, he shivered, remembering the chill of her presence. The way she'd loomed over him, steel-grey hair fixed in place, her dark blue eyes too like his for it to be a coincidence. He had the family eyes—no one had ever truly doubted whose son he was. Even if they didn't want to acknowledge the fact in public.

Liam shook off the memories and slipped back behind the steering wheel of his hire car.

Thornwood was his—a bequest he'd never expected, or wanted. The very idea of it filled him with a heavy apprehension. Thornwood Castle came with more than just history—it came with a legacy. An acceptance into a society that had cast him out before he was even born. People said that the class wars were over, that nobody cared about legitimacy or status of birth any more. Maybe that was true in some places, but Liam knew that those prejudices were still alive and well in Thornwood.

Or they had been when Rose was alive. Now she was gone...

Could Thornwood be a home? All he remembered of it

was cold, unwelcoming halls and the obvious disapproval of his great-aunt's butler as he'd met him at the door.

But then there was the letter. The spidery, wavering handwriting on thick creamy paper that had come with the lawyer who'd explained the bequest. The letter from Rose, written just days before she'd died, asking him to make Thornwood Castle his home, at last. To finally take on the family legacy.

You may find it rather different than you recall...

That was what she'd written. But from this distance it looked exactly like his memories of the place. Grey, forbidding, unwelcoming.

Liam was pretty sure that wasn't what home was supposed to look like.

Although, in fairness, he could be wrong. He could barely remember having a real home at all. Since his mother died, he'd ricocheted among his reluctant relatives—first his mother's, out in Australia, then later a brief trip over to the UK to be rejected by his long departed father's odd, unknown family—and foster care, never finding anywhere to settle for long. And since he'd been out in the world on his own he'd been far too busy building the life he'd craved for himself—one based on his own merits, not who he was related to—to worry about building that home of his own he'd dreamt of as a child.

He had the success he'd wanted. No one in his world knew him as the bastard son of the heir to an earldom, or even as Marie's poor little orphaned boy. These days he was known as his own man—a renowned and respected architect, owner of his own company, with turnover doubling every year. He was his own success story.

Maybe he could bring some of that success to Thornwood.

That was the plan, at least. The time for old-fashioned stately homes was over; nobody needed that much space any more. But that didn't mean he couldn't make Thornwood work for him. Tourists still had a fascination with the old British aristocracy—Liam's ex-girlfriend had watched enough period dramas for Liam to be sure of that. So if Thornwood was his it had to earn its keep—just like any other building he'd ever designed or renovated. Thornwood just had more potential than a lot of them.

And he couldn't help but smile out into the rain, just a little, at the thought of Great-Aunt Rose's face watching from above—or below, probably—seeing Thornwood turned into the sort of aristocratic theme park she'd always hated. He might not have known Rose well, but she'd made her feelings about the hoi polloi roaming around her ancestral grounds *very* clear. As clear as the fact she included him in that number, whoever his father was.

She'd hate everything he had planned. And that was pretty much reason enough to do it. Call it closure, maybe. Finally taking over the world that had rejected him as a child.

Then he could move on, find his *own* home instead of one that had been left to him because there was no one else. Preferably somewhere it didn't rain so damn much.

Liam stared up once more at the shadows of the crenellations in the grey and hazy light, the narrow windows and the aged stonework, and knew that he *would* stay, just as Rose had asked. But only long enough to close that chapter of his life for ever. To finally slam the door on the family who'd never wanted him.

Then he could return to his real life.

Liam started up the engine of the hire car again and, checking his mirrors, pulled back onto the road to drive the last half a mile up the long, winding driveway to the castle itself, smiling out through the windscreen at the rain as it started to fall in sheets.

He was nearly home, for now.

Alice Walters stared at the scene in front of her with dismay. 'What happened?' she asked as a couple of holly berries floated past on a stream that definitely didn't belong in the main hall of Thornwood Castle.

'Penelope was filling vases with water to add some of the greenery we collected from the woods,' Heather explained, arms folded tight across her chest. The frown that seemed to have taken up permanent residence on her forehead since Rose died looked even deeper than usual. 'Apparently she got distracted.'

'And forgot to turn off the tap.' It wasn't the first time that Penelope had got distracted. Alice supposed she should be used to it by now. 'Where's Danielle?'

'No idea,' Heather said, the words clipped. 'You know, for an assistant she doesn't seem to be very much help.'

Alice sighed. She'd noticed the same thing recently too. When she'd first hired the teenager to give her a hand with the admin and such at Thornwood, mostly to help her earn a part-time income after her mother died, Danielle had seemed bright and happy to be there. But over the last few months she'd barely even bothered showing up. 'Right, well, we'd better get the mops out. He'll be here any minute.'

'Our new lord and master,' Heather said, distaste obvious in her tone. 'I can't wait.'

'He might not be that bad.' Alice headed towards the nearest store cupboard and pulled out a mop and bucket. Given the number of leaks the castle roof had sprung over the last few years, they always tried to keep supplies close at hand. For a once grand house, the place leaked like a sieve and was impossible to keep warm. She wondered if the newest owner knew what he was letting himself in for. 'Rose wouldn't have left him the castle if he was.'

'Wouldn't she?' Heather took the mop from her and attempted to soak up some of the impromptu river, while Alice hunted for more rags and cloths to absorb the worst of it. 'He's the last of the line—illegitimate or not. It wouldn't matter *what* Rose thought about him. She'd leave him the castle because that's what tradition said she had to do. And you know how she felt about tradition—at least you should. You spent enough time arguing with her about it.'

'I did,' Alice said, sighing again. As if an indoor river wasn't bad enough, she had the prospect of spending her morning showing the new owner of Thornwood Castle around the wreck he'd inherited.

Rose might not have always been the easiest woman to get along with, but she'd been pragmatic, in the way that people who'd seen everything the world had to throw at them come and go, and leave them standing, often were. She might not have *liked* the suggestions that Alice put forward about how to keep the castle alive and running, but she'd been willing to grit her teeth and bear it, if it meant that her home, her family estate, would survive to be useful to another generation, as something more than a historical show-and-tell. More than anything, Alice was sure, Rose just hadn't wanted to be the one to let it go.

But what about her great-nephew? He was the unknown quantity. Would he care enough about Thornwood to work with them to keep it going? Or would he sell it to the first Russian oligarch who offered him seven figures for it?

Alice supposed she'd find out soon enough.

Not that it mattered to her. Not really. There was always work for a woman who could be organised, inventive, effective and productive—and Alice made sure that she was all those things. Rose had written her a glowing reference before she died, just in case she needed it. Alice would have no problem finding a new job—a new project to dive into and find a way to make it work. And it was getting time to move on—she'd already been at Thornwood longer than she'd planned. Normally she'd be looking forward to it. Except...

'Alice?' Penelope stuck her head around the door, her eyes huge and wide in her thin, pale face. Sixteen and already so disillusioned by life, Penelope—and all the other girls and women like her—was the only reason Alice was reluctant to leave Thornwood. The castle might not be her home, but it was the only place some of the women she helped had—and it was the best shot Alice had at doing something that mattered. Sure, she could get a job organising someone's office, or arranging meetings and scheduling flights. But here at Thornwood she was making a difference. And that counted for a lot.

'What is it, Penelope?' Alice asked when the girl didn't say anything further.

Slipping into the hall, Penelope wrapped her oversized grey cardigan around herself, her arms crossing over her middle. 'There's a car just pulled up. A big black four-by-four.' Her eyes slid away from Alice's as she spoke.

Alice and Heather exchanged a quick glance.

'That'll be him, then,' Heather said with a nod. 'Penelope, grab those cloths from Alice and do your best to mop up this mess, yeah? God knows where Danielle has got to.'

Penelope did as she was told, just like she always did—without question, without complaint, without a word. One day, Alice hoped that she might just look up and say, 'No.' One day.

Hopefully not today, though, as they really did need to clear up the mini flood.

Alice wiped her damp hands on her jeans. 'Right then. I'd better…' She flapped a hand towards the entrance hall.

Heather nodded. 'You go. Go meet the beast.'

Alice rolled her eyes. 'He might be lovely!'

'You keep telling yourself that,' Heather said, turning away to help Penelope with the remaining puddles. 'Just because I've never met a man yet who was, doesn't mean that this Liam bloke might not be the one who broke the mould.'

'Exactly,' Alice said, hoping she sounded more certain than she felt. 'And, at the very least, we have to give him a chance.'

She just hoped that he gave her—and Heather, and Penelope, and all the others—a chance too.

Grabbing his bag from the back seat, Liam pressed the button to lock the car and turned to face Thornwood Castle in the flesh for the first time in twenty-five years.

'Yeah, still imposing as all hell,' he murmured, eyeing the arrow slits.

As far as he'd been able to tell from the notes his assistant had put together on the castle, it had never really been built for battle. In fact, it was constructed about two hundred years too late for the medieval sieges and warfare it looked like it was built to withstand. It was more or less a folly—one of those weird English quirks of history. Some ancestor of his—by blood if not name or marriage—had got it into his head that he wanted to live in a medieval castle, even if it was the seventeen-hundreds. So he'd designed one and had it built. And then that castle had been passed down through generations of family members until it reached him, in the twenty-first century, when all those arrow slits and murder holes were even less necessary than ever.

Well, hopefully. He hadn't been back to Britain in a couple of years. Who knew what might have changed…?

Normally, Liam would happily mock the folly as typical aristocratic ridiculous behaviour. But as his assistant, Daisy, had pointed out to him drily as she'd handed him his plane tickets, building follies and vanity projects was basically what he did for a living these days. And he supposed she had a point. How was designing and building a hotel in the shape of a lily out in the Middle East any different to a medieval castle in the seventeen-hundreds?

Except he didn't keep the buildings he designed, or force them on future generations. He did an outstanding job, basked in the praise, got paid and moved on.

Much simpler.

As he jogged up the stone steps to the imposing front door, Liam tried to find that desert warmth again inside himself, and the glow of a good job well done. He was renowned these days, and in great demand as an architect. He'd built structures others couldn't conceive of, ones that every other architect he knew said was impossible.

There was no reason at all that he should still feel this intimidated by a fake English castle.

Straightening his shoulders, he reached out for the door handle—only to have it disappear inwards as the door opened by itself.

No, not by itself.

Liam blinked into the shadows of the entrance hall and made out one, two, three—five women standing there, blinking back at him.

For a moment he wondered if this was his staff—all lining up to meet him, as the new master. Even if he couldn't inherit the title that would have been his father's, if he'd lived long enough, he had the estate now.

Then he realised that the women were all wearing jeans

and woolly jumpers—and that, somehow, inside the castle felt even colder than outside.

'You must be Liam!' the woman holding the door said, beaming. 'I mean, Mr Howlett.'

'Jenkins,' he corrected her automatically. 'Liam Jenkins. I use my mother's name.' No need to explain that he'd never been offered his father's.

From the colour that flooded her cheeks, the woman knew that. 'Of course. I'm so sorry. Mr *Jenkins*.'

She looked so distraught at the slip-up, Liam shrugged, falling back into his usual pattern of making others feel comfortable. 'Call me Liam.'

'Liam. Right. Thank you.' The pink started to fade, which was a shame. Without it, she looked pale and cautious, her honey-blonde hair made dull by the grey light and shadows of the castle. But for that brief moment she'd looked…alive. Vibrant, in a way Liam hadn't expected to find at Thornwood.

Which still told him nothing about who she was or why she was in his castle. 'And you are…?'

'Oh! I'm Alice Walters. Your great-aunt hired me to, well, to make Thornwood Castle *useful* again.'

'Useful?' Liam frowned. 'It's a medieval castle in the twenty-first century. How *useful* can it really be?' Interesting, he could understand. Profitable, even more so. He'd half expected to find a guided tour in progress when he arrived—all the people who'd been kept out for so long coming to gawk at everything Rose had left behind. Nothing compared to what he had planned for the place. He had so many ideas for what to do to Thornwood—things he knew Great-Aunt Rose never would have even considered—to make the place into a proper tourist attraction. One he didn't have to visit, but still paid him handsomely.

He'd considered all sorts of options since he'd first got the phone call telling him that Thornwood Castle was his.

He just hadn't considered *useful*, beyond his own financial purposes.

'Rose wanted to make sure that the castle fulfilled its traditional role in the community,' Alice said vaguely. 'She hired me to make that happen.'

'Its traditional role?' He was starting to sound like a bad echo. But really, Alice's explanations weren't explaining anything at all.

Perhaps it was time for some non-English bluntness. After all, he was more Aussie than English when it came down to it—whatever Rose's will said.

'Look,' he said, taking care to sound more bored than annoyed, 'I'll make this really easy for you. Just a simple answer to a very simple question. What the hell are you all doing in my home?'

CHAPTER TWO

OKAY, THIS WAS not going as well as she'd hoped it might. Even if she hadn't really hoped all that hard—her experiences were generally even worse than Heather's, after all.

Behind her, she heard Penelope let out a tiny gasp at Liam's words and realised it was time to move this conversation elsewhere, before he upset *all* their girls. He might sound so laid-back he was almost horizontal, but this was his house and he could still throw them all out on a moment's notice if she didn't do something fast.

'Mr Jenkins, how about you come with me into the estate office? I can explain everything there.' Plus there was a kettle. And biscuits. Maybe a nice cup of tea and a sit down would make them all friends.

'Works for me,' he said with a shrug.

She led him the long way round—partly to avoid any remaining flooding in the great hall, and partly to show off some of the parts of Thornwood that *weren't* underwater.

'Has it been many years since you were last at Thornwood?' she asked politely as they skirted around the edges of the library, avoiding the combination of mismatched tables pushed together in the middle of the room with abandoned wool and knitting needles strewn across them. Everyone had dropped what they were doing the moment Liam's car had pulled up. Understandable, given the impact he stood to have on their future. But still, Alice couldn't help but wish they'd paused to tidy up a bit first.

'Twenty-five,' Liam said, raising his eyebrows at a ball of neon orange wool that had rolled off the table and into his path.

Alice swept it up as she passed, and lobbed it back on to the nearest table once he wasn't looking. Really, for an Australian, it seemed he had the imperious English aristocrat thing down pat. The mixture of relaxed disapproval was most disconcerting.

'That's a long time,' she said, knowing it sounded inane. But really, what else was she supposed to say?

Your great-aunt was alone for the last fifteen years of her life, and you couldn't even spare an afternoon to visit?

Sure, he lived on the other side of the world. But Alice had been doing some reading up on Liam Jenkins, ever since she'd got wind of the details of the will, and she was willing to bet he'd been in London often enough over those twenty-five years. Looking at his résumé, he'd built at least a handful of buildings less than two hours' drive away. How hard would it have been to stop in and see a lonely old lady? Or even to check on his inheritance, if he was truly that heartless.

Alice frowned. So why hadn't he? Having met him, she could buy him not being bothered enough about Rose to visit. But he'd called Thornwood Castle his home. How could it be home if he hadn't been there in two and a half decades? Maybe it was just a slip of the tongue. Or maybe not…

Suddenly, Alice got the feeling she was missing something in this story. It had the ring of the tales she'd heard from some of the women who stopped by the castle sometimes. Stories about slipping on the stairs, or losing their purse with the housekeeping money in it. No more believable than walking into a door and getting a black eye, but that was the point. Nobody expected those tales to be believed, not here. They didn't need to be. Thornwood was a safe place.

But maybe Liam didn't know that yet.

Well, if he wanted to make it his home, he'd have to learn. And hopefully he'd see the value of it, and let her continue her work.

Otherwise, there were going to be a lot of local women who didn't have a safe place any more.

With that dismal thought, they reached the estate office. Alice reached past the suit of armour she'd named Rusty and opened the door. 'Come on in.'

Inside, the office was as tidy as it ever got. Which, given that it was essentially a store cupboard with a desk shoehorned in and covered in a mass of paperwork and Post-it notes, wasn't very. Thornwood had plenty of rooms—far more than one person could ever need. But when Alice had arrived at the castle three years before, she'd known that all those public spaces could be put to better use. Besides, they were all far too big—echoing and full of draughts. At least here in her little cupboard she was cosy. And hardly anyone ever came looking for her there.

'Have a seat.' She motioned to the rickety wooden dining chair on the near side of the desk, and squeezed past the filing cabinet to flip on the kettle. She didn't need to look back to know he was staring dubiously at the seat— she'd done the same. Rose had said it dated back over a hundred years and hadn't collapsed yet. Alice thought it might just be biding its time.

Maybe it had been waiting for Liam Jenkins…

She turned back but the chair was still standing, even under Liam's weight. Which…well, he was a big man. Lots of muscle. Objectively, she supposed he could even be called well built, which was more than she'd have said for the chair before this point.

Maybe the chair was as scared of him as she was...

No. That was crazy—and not just because chairs didn't have emotions. She wasn't scared of Liam—he was too laconic to be scared of. She was...*apprehensive*, that was the word. And, even then, it was only because he could end everything that she'd built here in one fell swoop. It wasn't *personal.* He had no power to hurt her, not like other men had. He was her boss, and if he fired her she'd be fine and free to pursue other worthwhile projects elsewhere.

This wasn't like before. She had to remember that, even when he was scowling at her.

She wasn't that Alice any more, and she never would be again. That much she knew for sure. Life had changed her—not always for the better, but for ever.

'So,' Liam said as they waited for her ancient kettle to brew, 'what's the conversation we need to have that you couldn't have in front of all those women out there?'

'Not couldn't,' she corrected him. 'Chose not to.'

'Right.' He shrugged, obviously not seeing the difference. Alice sighed. Perhaps that was where she needed to start.

'Those women—they're part of the work I've been doing here,' she said, swilling hot water around the teapot to warm it. She might not have space for much in her utility cupboard office, but there was a sink, a kettle and a teapot with cups and saucers. Besides her laptop, there really wasn't much else that she needed.

'Yeah, your work. Making Thornwood *useful*, wasn't it?'

Did he really have to put such emphasis on the word? He made her sound like a small child trying to earn money for chores. 'How much do you know about the history of the English aristocracy, Mr Jenkins?'

'Not as much as you, I'd wager.' He watched her, curiosity in his gaze, as she measured out the tea leaves and added the boiling water, before leaving the tea to steep. 'I suppose you're going to educate me? Starting with the national drink?'

'I'm no expert myself,' Alice assured him. She placed the pretty floral cups and saucers on the tray beside the pot and the small milk jug, then swivelled round to place the whole thing on the desk. Settling into her own desk chair, she rested her forearms on the wood of the desk and eyed him over the steam drifting up from the spout of the teapot. 'But I know what that history meant to your great-aunt.'

'It meant she left me this place, for a start.'

'That's right.' However wrong a decision that might have been. Rose had been full of misgivings, Alice knew, about leaving Thornwood to someone she knew so little, who had shown no interest at all in his heritage or legacy before. But, when it came down to it, Liam Jenkins was the only family she had left. So blood had trumped legitimacy, and everything else that went with it. 'But I want to be sure you understand exactly the expectations that she was leaving with that. Thornwood is more than just a pile of stones and rusty armour, you know.'

'I know that,' Liam shot back, too fast to sound at all casual. 'It's home, right? My family pile, so to speak.'

There was that word again. Home. Obviously that mattered to him and, even if she never knew why, perhaps Alice could use it. Could appeal to his decency—didn't everyone deserve a home? Even those women out there whom he'd never met, who'd left hideously coloured wool all over the place and half flooded his castle?

It could work. Maybe.

Alice took a deep breath. She was going to have to try.

* * *

Liam eyed Alice over the desk and felt a small shiver of nerves at the back of his neck as she studied him back, then gave a tiny nod. She'd made a decision about something, that much was clear. He only wished he had the faintest clue what.

Alice, he was starting to realise, had plans for Thornwood—plans that were almost certainly at odds with his own. Which was why it was just as well *he* was the one who held the deeds to the castle, not her.

Maybe she was some sort of gold-digger. One who'd had his great-aunt wrapped around her little finger, taking advantage of her money and kindness—if the old bat really had any of either at the end—and expected to inherit. She must be furious to be done out of Thornwood, if that was the case. Good. He might not have deserved to inherit the place but, if she really was a gold-digger, she deserved it a thousand times less. And what was the deal with all those big-eyed women in cable knits?

'Rose believed, very strongly, that the privilege of owning a place like Thornwood, and the status in society that it conveyed, came with a very definite level of responsibility too,' Alice said, sounding so earnest that Liam almost put aside his gold-digger theory immediately. But only almost. After all, if she was good at it, of course she'd sound authentic. And, from what he remembered of Great-Aunt Rose, Alice would have had to be *very* good to fool her.

'A responsibility to the estate?' he guessed. Thornwood had been Rose's life—keeping it going would have been her highest priority. God, she must have shuddered as she'd signed the documents that meant it would come into his hands. But Alice's expression told him she meant more than that. So he kept guessing. 'Is this about the title? Or that seat in the House of Lords thing? Because I didn't inherit the title.' Even Rose wouldn't go so far as to convey that kind of status on the illegitimate son of her nephew. 'And besides, I heard that Britain finally moved with the times and stopped giving people power just because of who their parents were. Well, apart from that whole monarchy thing.'

Alice shook her head. 'It's not anything to do with the title, not really. Except that...' She sighed, as if the impossibility of making him understand her quaint British ways was beginning to dawn on her. 'In the past, the lord of the manor—or lady, in Rose's case—was responsible for the people who lived on their estate.'

'You mean feudalism,' Liam said with distaste. 'Just another word for slavery, really.' Just because he wasn't British didn't mean he wasn't educated. She looked slightly surprised to realise that.

'No! Not feudalism—at least, not for the last several hundred years. No, I just meant...the people who live on the estate have, traditionally, worked there too—usually as farmers. The local village is owned by the estate too, so it sets all the rents and has an obligation to take care of the tenants. They're more...extended family than just renters, if you see what I mean.'

'Yeah, I guess so.' It wasn't something he'd thought of before. He'd been so focused on the memory of Thornwood Castle's imposing walls, and the chilly reception the place had offered him, that he hadn't thought beyond the castle itself. He'd assumed that it would come with some gardens or whatever, but not a whole *village*. *That* was considerably more 'home' than Liam had bargained for, even if he didn't plan to stay. And how would they take the news that Thornwood Castle was about to become the county's biggest tourist attraction? He'd just have to spin it as good news—get them excited about the new jobs and tourist income before they realised how much disruption it would cause, or started getting nostalgic about the old days. Same as any other big project, really.

'So, what? They need me to open a village fete or something?' He'd seen the *Downton Abbey* Christmas special with his ex-girlfriend. That was practically a British documentary, right?

'Not exactly.' Alice looked uncomfortable but she pushed on regardless. Liam supposed he had to admire her determination to get her point across, whatever that point turned out to be. 'Times have changed around here. A lot of the farmland had to be sold off, and the village itself is pretty much autonomous these days. And Rose…well, as she got older, she couldn't get out and about so much. But she still wanted Thornwood Castle to be relevant. To be useful.'

There was that word again. 'And so she hired you. To do what, exactly?'

'To fundraise for and organise events that make the castle available to local women in need.' The words came out in a rush, and Liam blinked as he processed them over again, to make sure he'd heard her right.

'Like a refuge?' Because that was basically the last thing he'd expect from Great-Aunt Rose. After all, she hadn't even offered *him* a refuge when he'd needed one and he, whether she liked it or not, was her own flesh and blood.

Maybe Rose had changed over the years, but he doubted it. So what was he missing here? He guessed if anyone knew, it would be Alice. Which meant he needed to keep asking questions.

'Sort of,' she said, waggling her head from side to side. 'A lot of the girls and women we help, they don't feel they can spend a lot of time at home. So they come here instead.'

'They're abused?' Liam met her gaze head-on, looking for the truth behind her words. 'Then why don't you help them get out? Not just set them up with some knitting needles to make cardigans in some draughty castle?' He knew abuse; he'd seen it first-hand at some of the foster homes he'd been sent to. Suffered it too—both there and at home, with his mother's boyfriends.

But, more than that, he'd seen what it had done to *her*. It had broken his mother's spirit, if not her body. Somehow, he knew that it was the emotional and physical abuse that she'd suffered, the rejections and the hate, that had convinced her it wasn't worth fighting for life any longer. Medicine might not be able to prove it yet, but he knew in his bones that if she'd not felt so worthless she could have beaten the cancer that finally took her life when he was ten.

He could see it now—the fear behind the eyes of the women who'd met him at the door. He'd assumed it was just the uncertainty that came with his arrival, but he should have known better. Should have recognised what he saw. Had he been away from that world, safe in the land of money and prestige, for so long that he'd forgotten what fear looked like?

'We don't… Okay, yes, sometimes we hold classes and today's was knitting. But they don't knit their own cardigans.' She frowned. 'At least, not as far as I know. And that's not the point, anyway. You asked why we don't get them out of abusive situations. We do, if they're ready to go. We give them the support they need to make that decision, and put them in touch with the charities that can do it properly. But for some of them…' Alice sighed. 'The women and girls who come here, they all have their own stories, their own lives, their own individual situations. Some aren't abused; they just need something else in their lives. Some are still torn about what to do for the best—

for their kids, for themselves. And it's easy for us to say, "You need to get out, now." But sometimes it takes them a while to see that.'

'So you just set up craft classes to distract them from all the things that are wrong in their lives?' Fat lot of good that would do anyone.

Alice glared at him. 'So we provide educational opportunities—computer classes, job interview training, talks from the local college about what courses are available, that sort of thing. We help rewrite CVs, we run food banks for those local families struggling to make ends meet, or clothes swaps and donations to provide school uniforms or interview clothes, we help decipher benefits claims forms, we hold meditation groups, exercise classes, cooking classes, breastfeeding workshops for new mums, help with childcare…everything we can think of that will make everyday life easier or provide new opportunities for the women and families of this village. And if they need to get out of a situation, we help them do that too. And we do it all on donations, persuading people to volunteer their time, and by making do with what we have. So no, it's not just knitting.'

Her eyes were blazing now, her cheeks red and her pale hair had frizzed a little in the steam from the tea—or her anger. And Liam realised, with a sudden, sinking certainty, that Alice Walters wasn't a gold-digger. She was something much worse—for him, at least.

Alice Walters was a do-gooder. A determined, stubborn, dedicated doer of good. And while he might admire that kind of zeal in someone else, right now he was mentally cursing it. Not because he didn't want to help all those women—he did. That was the problem.

Because his vision for Thornwood Castle, his big middle finger to the society and family that had rejected him, sure as hell didn't include groups of troubled women and kids tramping around his personal space, while Alice harangued him to give more, help more, do more. He could see it now—a supplier meeting interrupted by a crying woman, or a visionary design lost to some child's scribbles.

They couldn't stay, that much was obvious. But he couldn't just throw them out either. It wasn't that she'd got to him or anything, with her speeches about safe places and refuge and need. But if Thornwood had become essential to the local community, he needed to convince the local community—and, more importantly, Alice—that their needs would be better served elsewhere, so he could get on with his own plans.

That, he suspected, might take time. Well, time he had—Thornwood had stood for this long waiting for him; it would last a little longer while he sorted all this out. The castle would be his, and only his, eventually. Liam Jenkins was renowned in business for always getting what he wanted—no matter how long it took.

But for now the only thing to do was to gauge exactly what he was up against. And whether he could buy his way out of it.

Reaching for a biscuit for the road, he said, 'You're right. I had no idea of the scope of your work here. Why don't you show me round the place while you tell me more about the work you do and the fundraising you've got going on?'

At least the surprise on her face was a small consolation for the work he had ahead of him.

CHAPTER THREE

THE MAN WAS *impossible* to read. Alice had always heard that Australians were open and honest, friendly but blunt. Clearly Liam had more of his father's side in him than his upbringing would suggest, because he was giving *nothing* away. Every relaxed shrug or bland stare hid his thoughts all too effectively.

He'd nodded politely as she'd shown him around the bedrooms, barely even acknowledging the King's room, where past monarchs had slept. She supposed that the history of the crown might not mean that much to him, but she'd expected at least a flicker of appreciation at the giant four-poster bed, or even just the place Thornwood held in the heart of the nation. Still, nothing.

'And do the women ever stay over here?' he asked as she shut another bedroom door.

'Sometimes,' Alice admitted. 'Not often, because even with this many bedrooms if we started setting up some sort of bed and breakfast we'd be swamped in days. We simply don't have the resources—and, to be honest, a lot of the bedrooms aren't really in a suitable condition for guests.'

'No beds?'

'No heating. Or insulation. Or glass in the windows, in some cases.' She shivered. 'Thornwood in winter is not a warm place.'

'Hence the cardigans.' What *was* his obsession with knitwear? Alice wondered, as Liam strode off down the hallway. He had a good stride, she couldn't help but notice. Strong, muscled legs under his trousers, a long step and a purposeful gait. He looked like a man who was there to get a job done.

Alice just wished she had some idea what the job at hand was, for him. Because *obviously* he had plans. A man like Liam Jenkins didn't just show up at Thornwood Castle with a vague dream of medieval re-enactments or something.

'So, which room is yours?' Liam called back, and Alice scurried to catch him up.

'Um, I have a box room on the ground floor.' Near the boiler, and close to the kitchens. It was the warmest place in the castle, and Alice loved it—even if it wasn't all that much bigger than her office. Small spaces were comforting. There was no space for anything—or anyone—to hide, there.

'Rose had the master suite, along here, though,' she added, taking a left turn in the corridor and leading him to a large oak door. 'We've cleared it out already, and it's made up fresh if you'd like to use it?' She hoped so. Rose's suite was one of the few bedrooms in a suitable condition for long-term accommodation. If he said no, Alice had a feeling it would somehow become her job to clear out and do up another room to suit him.

Somehow, a lot of things around Thornwood became Alice's job, mostly just because it was quicker and easier to take care of things herself than expect anyone else to do it.

Actually, not just around Thornwood. Alice's rule for living number two was: don't expect anyone to do anything for you. She figured if they did it was a pleasant surprise. And at least she was never disappointed when they inevitably didn't.

Technically, Rose had hired her as a fundraiser—to raise money to help keep Thornwood running, without having to open it up for tours. Alice had convinced her that the best way to keep the house open, useful and sort of private was to use it to help the local residents. Rose's sense of duty had been tickled, and now here they were. Alice raised money—through begging phone calls to donors, or fundraising activities on site—but she also organised the seminars and classes they held, as well as took care of the women. Her salary—small as it was—was paid from the money she raised, so she rarely took more than her room and board, and money for essentials. She was all too aware of the other uses that money could be put to.

Everyone else on site was a volunteer—except for Maud, the cook-slash-housekeeper, who'd been in Rose's service for decades. Even Heather, who practically ran the place when Alice was busy, did it for nothing. And she had quickly claimed responsibility for taking care of the women who came to them in real trouble, which Alice appreciated. They'd managed to put together a stockpile in the pantry, full of all the essentials women, children and babies might need—especially if they couldn't go home again. Some just needed enough food to see them through until payday. Others needed clothes, toiletries, nappies, a pay-as-you-go phone with a number no one had—and a way out. Alice was proud that their work meant they could help all of them—or at least get them to the best place for them to find real long-term help. She'd built up great connections with refuges and charities nationwide, and the work they did at Thornwood was well respected. Women came to them now from across the county, not just the local villages.

She just hoped Liam's sense of duty was as strong as his great-aunt's.

Opening the door to the suite of rooms, she let Liam walk in first, ignoring the slight pang in her chest she always felt when she saw Rose's space empty.

Alice couldn't honestly say that she and Rose had been friends, but she had certainly developed a great deal of respect for the old woman in the time she'd been working at Thornwood. Rose's beliefs and opinions might have been from a bygone age in lots of ways, but when it came down to the essentials she was practical and—to Alice's great surprise—compassionate.

Rose could have sold Thornwood for millions twice over, or she could have hired a company to make it into a tourist attraction. But instead she'd hired Alice, and told her to 'make Thornwood useful again'. Not in a large, flashy, lucrative way. In a way that served the community, and filled a gap in society. In a way that helped people— women just like Alice had been four years ago. Desperate.

Leaning against the heavy door, she watched Rose's great-nephew explore the room—running a hand over the antique dresser, sticking his head into the more modern bathroom. Then he crossed to the window and stared out at the gardens beyond.

'What do you think?' Alice asked when he didn't turn back. 'Will it suit?'

'Hmm?' Liam turned back, apparently startled out of his own thoughts. 'Oh, definitely. The space out there will be perfect for—' He cut himself off. 'You meant the rooms. Yeah, they'll be fine. I don't imagine I'll be spending much time in them, anyway.'

Which begged the question—where *was* he planning on spending his time? And doing what? Because he sure as hell hadn't been thinking about the bedroom when he'd been looking out of that window. He'd been making plans—plans he clearly had no intention of sharing with *her*.

And that made Alice very nervous indeed.

'Ready to show me downstairs?' Liam flashed her a smile, as if the last few moments hadn't happened at all.

Alice narrowed her eyes. He was hiding something, that much was clear. But what? And how much harm could it do to everything Alice had built up at Thornwood?

She supposed there was only one way to find out.

She took a deep breath and stretched her face into a bright and happy smile. 'Absolutely.'

Liam followed Alice back down endless, labyrinthine corridors, still thinking about the large expanse of forest he'd seen from Rose's window. It would be perfect for an outdoor pursuits centre. He could see go-karting and paintball, maybe a ropes course. Plenty to keep the kids entertained while the parents took high tea up at the castle, or whatever it was people wanted from a stately home. Regardless, there was plenty of potential there.

Once he'd dealt with the castle's *current* residents, of course.

After one last sharp turn in the corridor, they were suddenly spat out into a wide-open landing, leading to a grand double staircase, which joined halfway down to provide steps wider than he was tall. The dark wooden bannisters had been twined with glossy dark green leaves and bright red berries. Below stood an enormous Christmas tree, already strung with lights and glass baubles, the angel on top almost reaching the very top of the stairs. Liam couldn't imagine how they'd even got it in through the doors.

'Impressive tree,' he said, nodding towards it.

Alice gave him a small, tight smile. 'We like to celebrate life every way we can here. Now, after you?' She gestured towards the stairs.

Liam frowned. The staircase was clearly wide enough for both of them to descend at the same time, yet Alice hung back in a way she hadn't before. She was the one who knew her way around, so she'd led the way for most of the tour. What was different now? Was this some sort of prank?

He took the first step gingerly, relieved when it felt perfectly solid and ordinary under his foot.

Behind him, he heard Alice let out a long breath of relief, and knew that this was just another puzzle he'd need to figure out before he could leave Thornwood.

Safely at the bottom, Liam turned to admire the staircase. It would be a grand welcome for guests, a great way to make them feel they really had bought a piece of the English aristocracy experience. Then he blinked, and realised he wasn't looking at the staircase at all.

He was watching Alice.

She skipped down the stairs easily enough, one hand bouncing along the bannister in between the greenery. The tension he'd heard in her voice when she asked him to go first was gone, and instead she looked…what? Guarded, maybe? As if there was something here she was trying to hide—something more than leaky ceilings and missing windows. Something other than just Thornwood.

Something about *her.*

He frowned as she reached the ground floor and glided across to straighten an ornament on the tree. Why, exactly, had Alice Walters come to Thornwood in the first place? He'd assumed she'd just been an eccentric hire of Rose's, but now he was wondering. Obviously she had to be good at her job, and have great organisational skills, if she was keeping all the courses and sessions running that she claimed—even if her office was a bomb site. And Rose had never had any patience for slackers, so she must be a hard worker. Not to mention good at eliciting donations, to pay for everything.

Those sorts of skills could command a significant wage in the business world—far higher than he could imagine Rose paying her. So what kept her at Thornwood? Was it just the desire to do good—and, if it was, what had instilled that need in her?

Or, and this seemed like more of a possibility than he'd previously considered, was *Alice* one of the women who had needed the safe haven of Thornwood?

For some reason the idea filled him with horror—far more than the usual pity or anger he'd expect at a women being caught in such a situation. The idea of Alice—fired up, determined, intense Alice—being diminished by someone, a man, he assumed… That was unacceptable.

She turned to him, her bright smile firmly back in place and her honey-blonde hair bouncing around her shoulders. Suddenly, she didn't look like a victim to him any longer. She looked like a strong, capable woman—one he needed to negotiate with before he could move on with his plans.

He was here for business, not to save people. Besides, he'd never been any good at that, anyway. He hadn't been able to save his mother, had he? And for every fight he'd got in the middle of, how many of the people he'd protected had just gone back and got beaten up again the next day? Probably most of them.

Better to focus on what he *was* good at—designing buildings and making them a success. *That* he knew how to do—even if Thornwood was a little different to his usual projects.

And Alice was a lot different to his usual challenges.

* * *

Relief settled over Alice as she saw that the river from that morning had been thoroughly mopped up and the main hall was looking its usual impressive self again, ready for its new owner. The Christmas tree appeared perfectly festive, as did the garlands on the banisters. And hopefully Liam hadn't noticed anything odd about her behaviour by the stairs—although, given how observant he seemed about other things, she wouldn't like to place a bet on it. Still, even if he *had* noticed, why would he care? He wasn't likely to worry about it enough to ask questions and find out what her problem was.

People usually didn't, in Alice's experience. No one wanted the second-hand trauma and misery of another person when they were already dealing with their own.

'Right, well, let's start in the library,' she said, forcing a bright smile. Hopefully someone might have even tidied up the knitting stuff by now, since a new session had been due to start ten minutes ago.

The library was one of Alice's favourite spots in the whole castle. The walls were lined with books, as one might expect, but Alice had brought her own touches to the place since she'd arrived, with Rose's blessing. While three walls still boasted shelves laden with dusty, oversized hardback tomes on subjects no one had experienced a need to research in decades, possibly centuries, the fourth wall had been transformed over the last year and a half. The dark wood shelves were now stuffed full of more modern books—self-help classics, career advice books, parenting and childcare publications, not to mention shelf after shelf of fiction. Alice had made sure to collect a good range, mostly from second-hand bookshops on her fundraising travels, so they had romance, detective stories, fantasy and sci-fi, thrillers, as well as a good selection of the classics and award-winners. Something for everybody, Alice liked to think.

Today, now that the knitting class had finished, there was a group huddled around the central tables discussing interview techniques. Alice and Liam hung back at the door rather than interrupt, and listened to the questions the women were posing.

'But what do I say when they ask why I've been out of work for so long?' one woman asked, leaning across the table.

Melanie, the careers adviser Alice had persuaded to come in and run the session for free, leaned back slightly. 'Well, I think the best plan is to be honest. Explain what you've been doing instead.'

'What? Changing nappies and mopping up spit-up?' The woman laughed. 'Why would they care about that?'

'Because everything you do, every day, is what shapes you.' Alice startled as Liam spoke, and the whole room turned towards him. Men at Thornwood were a rarity these days, for obvious reasons. One or two of the women looked a little anxious. Several more looked appreciative—Alice decided not to speculate if that was because of his advice or his appearance.

Liam stepped forward into the room, placing his hands on the back of an empty chair as he spoke. 'Any company worth working for knows that previous experience isn't the most important thing for a potential employee to have.'

'Then why do they all ask for it?' Jess, one of the younger women, asked.

'Oh, they'd like it, sure,' Liam acknowledged. 'But what they really need is someone who can learn. Someone who can walk into an interview and show them that they're bright, they're willing and, most importantly, they're enthusiastic. If you can make them believe that you'll work well with their team, listen and learn what you need to know, then go on to make the most of every opportunity they give you—and benefit their company along the way— then they'd be fools not to hire you.'

'So…you're saying it's all about the right attitude?' Jess said, frowning. 'Not qualifications and stuff?'

'Ninety per cent of the time, yes.' Liam shrugged. 'Yes, there are some roles that require specific qualifications, but they're fewer than you might think. And a lot of companies will train you up and help you get those qualifications, if they like you, and if they believe you'll make the most of the opportunity.'

'Huh.' Jess's frown transformed into a wide smile that lit up her whole face. Alice didn't think she'd ever seen that expression on Jess's face before. She rather suspected that it might be hope.

Suddenly, she felt considerably warmer towards Liam Jenkins. Anyone who could put that expression on the face of someone who'd been through as much as Jess had, well, he had to be worth keeping around.

Melanie thanked Liam for his input, and Alice hoped her feathers weren't too ruffled. It was hard enough finding people willing to give up their free time to run the sessions at Thornwood, especially since she could rarely offer them more than lunch as payment.

'Shall we carry on?' Alice asked, and Liam nodded.

'I hope I didn't overstep my place there,' he said as they made their way down the echoing stone corridor.

Alice gave him a lopsided smile. 'The whole estate is sort of your place,' she pointed out. 'You'd have to step a long way to get over your boundaries.'

From the stunned look on his face, Alice guessed he hadn't thought of it like that before. Maybe Liam was going to find this adjustment as odd as the rest of them.

'Well, when you put it like that…' He shook his head. 'I guess it's still sinking in. I never expected to inherit Thornwood. Not in a million years. The idea that I own all this, that it's all *mine*, as far as you can see from those replica battlements… That's going to take some getting used to.'

'Rose never spoke to you about her will?' Alice asked, surprised.

Liam shrugged. 'I hadn't seen her in fifteen years. And I hadn't been near Thornwood for a decade before that. And when we did meet…let's just say there were other things to discuss.'

What other things? Alice was desperate to know, but the way Liam looked away, his expression closing up, she knew better than to ask. Not yet, anyway. Maybe when she got to know the new lord of the manor a little better she'd feel more confident about such questions.

Maybe she'd understand what it was about him that made her need to know the answers too.

Still, for him to not even know he stood to inherit Thornwood…that was strange. Rose had wanted everything settled in the last year or two of her life—that was one of the reasons she'd hired Alice when she did. Everything had been arranged for months before she died. So why wouldn't she have told him? And even before that…

'But you were her only living relative. You must have known that Thornwood would naturally come to you,' Alice said, knowing she was pushing but unable to stop herself.

'Why?' Liam's voice grew hard. 'She'd never given me anything else I was entitled to, so the idea of her starting with Thornwood was kind of ludicrous.'

Alice stumbled slightly as she processed his words and, fast as a shot, Liam's hand caught her arm, steadying her. 'Sorry,' she gasped, trying not to react to the sudden flare of heat that ran through her at his touch. She was absolutely *not* going to develop anything approaching a crush on this man. That way lay madness, frustration and probably a whole load of embarrassment.

'Uneven floor,' Liam said, peering down at the stone under their feet. 'I'll have to get that fixed before—' He broke off.

'Before?' Alice asked, curious. What exactly did he have planned for Thornwood, anyway? Whatever it was, she got the distinct impression it wouldn't involve knitting groups.

'Before someone hurts themselves more seriously.' Liam dropped his hand from her arm and kept walking.

Alice studied him as she followed, rubbing the spot where he'd held her arm. It was a neat enough cover, but Alice had plenty of experience with dishonest men.

And Liam Jenkins was most definitely hiding something.

'So, where's next?' Liam asked, changing the subject quickly.

'Um…the kitchens?'

'Sounds great.' Liam started walking. He wasn't entirely sure where the kitchens were, but the fantastic scents wafting towards him suggested he was going the right way. And at least if he kept moving Alice would hopefully be distracted enough not to notice his less than smooth cover-up.

Obviously he'd need to explain his plans to her, and everyone else, eventually—making a big splash and putting the English establishment up in arms was part of the reason he was doing it in the first place—the rest, of course, being money. But he wanted to do it in his own time, and in a way that would have maximum impact. Alice gossiping about it to the locals in the village was definitely not that.

He frowned as Alice caught him up and said, 'This way,' as she took a sharp left turn. She didn't seem like the gossipy sort, he had to admit. In fact, she seemed like the sort of woman who could keep others' secrets as well as her own—and, even on an hour or two's acquaintance, Liam was sure she had plenty of those. But then, so did he. And if he wasn't planning on sharing, there was no reason she should.

If he handled this right, Alice wouldn't be around long enough for him to worry about her secrets, anyway.

'Here we are.' Alice stopped in front of a giant wooden door, arched at the top, and reached for the huge iron ring that served as a doorknob. As she turned it and pushed open the door, the wonderful aromas Liam had been enjoying hit him at full strength, along with a heat that was sorely absent from the rest of the castle. Roasting meat and onions and deep savoury smells that made his stomach growl with hunger. He half expected to see a roast pig on a spit over a roaring fire.

But when he looked past Alice, instead of the rustic brick and wood kitchen he was expecting, Liam found a shining modern one, complete with range cooker and a very efficient-looking woman in an apron. In fact, it looked set up to cater for the masses.

'Liam, this is Maud,' Alice said, motioning towards the cook. 'She was Rose's cook and housekeeper for twenty years, and she's very kindly stayed on to help us keep the place up and running. Maud, this is the new owner of Thornwood, Liam Jenkins.'

Maud wiped her hand on her apron before holding it out for him to shake. 'Pleasure, I'm sure.' Something in her tone told him that she wasn't at all sure, actually, but he appreciated the attempt at civility all the same. She turned away again, back to the pot on her hob.

'This is an impressive kitchen,' he said appreciatively. It was always good to get in with the person who was in charge of the food, he'd found.

'It's functional,' Maud said without looking at him. 'But to be honest, I prefer the Old Kitchen.'

'Old Kitchen?' Liam asked. 'I know this place is huge, but how many kitchens does it really need? This one looks like it could cater for pretty much any function you wanted to hold here.'

Alice laughed, the sound high and bright—but nervous, somehow. 'The Old Kitchen is *really* old. Like a period piece. We use it when we do family days, to show the kids how they used to make different food and drinks here in the past. We've done medieval days, Victorian days, all sorts. It's much more atmospheric than using the new kitchen, but this is better for when we have lots of people to feed.'

'Which seems like most of the time,' he observed.

'The Old Kitchen wouldn't be any good for all those fiddly canapés and such you like for your fundraisers, any-way,' Maud grumbled as she placed two plates of food on the counter before them. 'I'm going to be wrapping Parma ham around asparagus for days, I know it, to be ready for next Thursday.'

Beside him, Liam saw Alice wince. 'Next Thursday?'

'I was…going to mention that. We had planned a fund-raiser for next week. It's been in everyone's diaries for months, long before we knew Rose wouldn't be here to host it. We have some great pledges of support already. It would be such a shame to cancel it now…'

The question she wasn't asking hung in the heavily scented air between them. Would the fundraiser still be able to go ahead, now he was in charge?

Liam considered. On the one hand, what was the point?

Things were going to change around here, and he might as well start now. On the other, for his first act as the new owner of Thornwood to be cancelling a fundraiser for local women and children in need… That didn't send a great message.

'Fine. You can have your fundraiser,' he said, and Alice clapped her hands and grinned.

'Fantastic! I just know you'll be a great host. You did bring your dinner jacket, right?'

Wait. What? Liam had a sinking feeling that he'd just signed up for far more than he'd intended to—and that getting Alice Walters out of his castle might not be as easy as he'd hoped.

CHAPTER FOUR

'OKAY, I THINK we need to move that table back across to the other side,' Alice said. The women she'd roped in to help her set up for the fundraiser glared at her. 'Last time, I promise.'

As the table got moved across the ballroom, Alice rubbed her forehead to try to fend off a headache, and ticked off another item on her clipboard. The checklist was almost done, at last. It had been a long few days of preparation—not entirely helped by Liam sticking his nose in every few hours to see exactly what she was doing.

Thornwood Castle's new owner had been in residence for almost a week now, and he was certainly making his presence felt. Alice had hoped, when he'd agreed to let them go ahead with the fundraiser, that it was a sign he was happy for Thornwood to carry on as it always had.

Apparently not.

Over the past week, Liam had shown up to observe various classes, taken lunch with the women and kids in the dining hall, climbed up into the attics to inspect the roof, been observed checking and annotating the castle blueprints, and spent a day exploring the woods on the edge of the estate. The rest of the time he'd spent working in the room he'd claimed as his office, between the library and the kitchens, making phone calls, typing on his laptop or just talking to himself as he paced. Reporting back to Alice on what the new owner was up to had become a full-time game for the kids who hung around the castle after school. It was almost as if she had her own team of spies—even if she didn't have a clue what to do with the information they brought her.

Worst of all, whenever Alice had asked Liam if she could assist him at all, he'd just shrugged and smiled and said, 'Nah. It's all good. Just getting a feel for the place.'

It was making Alice very nervous.

'He's so infuriatingly laid-back,' she'd said to Heather, after another one of his 'don't mind me' visits to a first aid class she was giving.

Heather had laughed. 'Have you ever considered that maybe you're just too tense?'

Alice had glared at her, and gone back to doing her job. Mostly because she had no idea what else to do.

At least preparing for the fundraiser had given her something else to focus on, besides whatever plans Liam was hatching for Thornwood. If this was to be her last big event at the castle, she wanted to make it a good one.

The guest list was solid, she knew—she had the mayor, a couple of local councillors, a local celebrity chef and a duke and duchess from the next county, along with the usual bunch of lawyers, teachers, doctors and local businessmen and women. Maud had laid out a great spread, and Alice had ordered in plenty of champagne so that the bids in the silent auction should go high enough to make the evening worthwhile. Spending so much on one event always made her nervous, but she'd never failed yet to make back at least four times what she spent in donations and auction bids. She just had to keep reminding herself that all the glitz, glamour and fuss were worthwhile.

Even if she did have to wear a stupid, shiny dress with a desperately uncomfortable strapless bra.

'How's it going?' Alice spun at the sound of Liam's voice and found him casually leaning against the giant double doors of the ballroom, his arms folded across that broad chest.

'Fine! All fine,' she said, forcing a wide smile. She glanced around the ballroom. The tables were set up with the best cloths, and her helpers were laying out the silver and glass flatware. There were candles in the candelabras that would illuminate the room, ready to be lit nearer the start time. The floor had been polished, and the string quartet was tuning up in the corner. All she had left to do was set up the stuff for the silent auction, and get herself ready to schmooze and smile for the night.

'Looks good.' Liam nodded, lazily pushing away from the door and crossing the ballroom towards her. 'Want to tell me what I'm expected to do tonight?'

Alice nodded. 'Of course. Um, mostly it's just about chatting to people. You're new, so *everyone* is going to want to talk to you. They're going to want to know your plans for Thornwood, for a start.'

'Are they, indeed? Well, they might be disappointed on that one.'

'Because you don't have any firm plans yet?' Alice said hopefully. If he wasn't set on one course of action, she still had time to sway him towards her point of view.

Liam gave her a wolfish smile. 'Because I never share my plans until they're finalised.'

Damn. 'Well, I'm sure you'll manage. Other than that… it would be great if you could do a welcome toast. Just a "Thanks for coming, it's a great cause, raising money for the work being done here at Thornwood"—that sort of thing.'

'Sure,' Liam said, shrugging. 'What's the name?'

'The name?'

'Your centre, refuge, whatever we're calling it. What's the name? So I can tell people exactly what they're donating to.'

'It… Well, it doesn't really have a name,' Alice admitted. It had never needed one. Word just got around that Thornwood was a safe place. Sometimes they advertised some of their classes at the local doctors' surgeries and schools and such. But other than that…a name would make it official. Permanent. And Alice wasn't ready to commit to that sort of permanence—especially now.

'You should give it a name. People like to know exactly what they're giving to.' Liam checked his watch. 'And now I guess I'd better go put that monkey suit on.'

Alice's eyes widened as she clocked the time. How had it got so late? 'And I'd better go get changed.' And check in on Maud, and the servers she'd hired and the quartet and the auction and…

Breathe, Alice.

She'd done this six times or more before. She knew what she was doing. Everything would be fine.

Liam flashed her another smile, looking as relaxed and unbothered as could be, and Alice resisted the urge to throttle him. Just once, she'd like to see him riled up about something.

Except that something would probably be throwing her out of the castle. So never mind.

'I'll see you at the shindig,' Liam said. 'Save me a drink.'

'Will do.' Alice gave him a weak smile and watched him go.

Then she grabbed her clipboard and raced towards her box room to get ready.

It was almost time for the schmoozing to begin.

* * *

Liam's bow tie was strangling him. Oh, he knew that the networking and the dressing-up were all part of doing business these days, but usually he was talking about his work, his buildings. Not some ancient castle that still didn't feel like his.

He'd spent the last week trying to familiarise himself with the estate he'd unexpectedly inherited. He'd explored the grounds, the house, checked blueprints and restrictions, talked to lawyers and contractors, and kept tabs on the day-to-day activities of the castle. And finally, after days of note-taking and brainstorming and thinking out loud, he thought he might have found a solution to what he'd taken to calling The Alice Problem.

He couldn't throw out women and children in need. But he couldn't let them stay either. It was a conundrum.

He smiled to himself. Luckily, he'd always liked puzzles.

Now, he just needed to get Alice alone to persuade her to go along with it.

But first he'd discharge all his duties at this fundraiser, show willing, and hopefully get her guard down. The woman had been tense as anything since the moment he'd arrived—he'd assumed it was to do with him initially, but now he was starting to think it might be her natural state of being. Perhaps a glass or two of champagne—and a few fat cheques from the partygoers—would help her loosen up.

Snatching another glass of his own from the tray of a passing waiter, Liam smiled pleasantly at an older woman obviously wanting to talk to him, then managed to side-step away before she reached him. He'd already spoken with enough people for one night, and that wasn't even counting his toast.

All he wanted to do now was get Alice alone and get

the deal done—and then kick all these people out of his castle so he could get some peace and quiet.

Making his way over to the secret auction table, he busied himself by pretending to study the offerings—which varied from afternoon tea with the Duke to a weekend on somebody's yacht. Nothing he was at all interested in. Instead, he took the opportunity to scan the room, looking for Alice.

She'd done a great job, he had to admit. The ballroom was transformed from the Thornwood he'd become familiar with over the last week—no knitwear and screaming children, for a start. Not that he had anything against the kids—they were a lot more fun than most of the stuffed shirts in attendance tonight.

Looking around him, he could almost believe he was in a period drama. The chandeliers glittered, rivalling the sparkle from the diamonds and gemstones on display on the women in the room. The string quartet played the same pieces musicians had been playing at these events for centuries, and the usual small talk and chatter rose up to the high ceilings, along with the clinking of glasses. Maud's canapés—so different to the hearty fare she'd been feeding him, and everyone else, for the past week—were gobbled down with delight by all the partygoers. Liam had to admit, they were delicious. But they weren't a patch on the roast they'd had for dinner the night before.

His stomach rumbled, and he doubled his search for Alice. He'd seen her earlier, draped in a golden dress that left her shoulders and arms bare, and clung to her slender curves before flaring out over her hips. He'd actually done a double take at the sight of her—that dress was a far cry from the jeans and jumpers he was more used to seeing her in.

Really, she should be impossible to miss, looking like that. So where the hell was she?

Ah! There—off to one side, deep in conversation with a couple who'd cornered him earlier and talked for twenty minutes about the local sewage system. Well, she'd worked very hard on tonight. The least he could do was rescue her from *that*.

Then maybe they could go and find some real food—and talk.

Alice couldn't quite decide whether to be thankful that Liam had saved her from the death by boredom that was conversation with Mr and Mrs Haywood, or annoyed that he'd dragged her away from the fundraiser she'd spent months organising.

'I really shouldn't stay away too long,' she said as she followed Liam down the corridor away from the ballroom. 'We need to announce the winners of the silent auction soon…'

'Heather's going to do it,' Liam said, not even glancing back. 'I spoke to her before we left.'

'Really?' She was about to ask what gave him the right to do that, before she realised that they were actually in *his* castle, and bit her tongue. 'And what do we need to do that's so much more important than my fundraiser?'

Liam flashed her a smile over his shoulder as they reached the kitchen doors. 'Find some real food.'

Well. She supposed she could get behind that, Alice decided, her stomach rumbling. Two and a half canapés did not make a dinner.

'Plus, I have some plans I want to run by you,' Liam added, and Alice's appetite faded. For a moment, anyway.

Since the New Kitchen had been taken over by canapés and serving staff, they edged cautiously around the outside, avoiding Maud's glare as she directed the hired waiters and loaded them up with trays.

'Where do you think she's hidden last night's leftovers?' Liam asked, his mouth close to Alice's ear to be heard over the din. Alice tried not to shiver at the sensation of his breath on her skin.

'Probably in the mini fridge next door, in the Old Kitchen.'

'Then let's go.' Grabbing her hand, Liam led her towards the second door that led through to the old-fashioned second kitchen space.

Alice pushed open the door between them and felt, as she always did, as if she'd stepped back in time. The scrubbed wooden table with low benches on either side, the open fire with cooking pots hanging beside it, the maids' aprons and caps behind the door…everything harked back to an earlier age. A previous incarnation of Thornwood Castle.

She crossed to the smaller, out of place fridge that Maud kept in there, and wondered if she was about to hear what the latest incarnation would be.

Liam grabbed a couple of the old stoneware plates from the large dresser that covered one wall and placed them on either side of the table. Alice pulled out dishes of leftovers and laid them out in the centre, before rooting around to find cutlery for them both.

Liam folded himself on to one of the long benches that sat on either side of the kitchen table. Alice followed suit, sweeping her golden dress under her as she sat facing him. She handed him a set of cutlery, gripping her own so tightly that her knuckles turned white.

'You don't need to look so tense,' Liam said, his Australian accent and mild tone making his words sound even more laid-back.

'Don't I?' Alice asked. 'I mean, you're about to tell me your plans for the future of this place, right?' She hoped so, anyway. Otherwise she'd read him totally wrong, and things were about to get worse, not better.

Oh, hell, what if he was just about to fire her on the spot, not discuss his plans? She hoped he'd let her finish her dinner first—even cold, Maud's roasts always tasted amazing.

Liam chuckled, as if he'd read her mind. 'Eat. We'll talk when we're both done. I never like to negotiate on an empty stomach.'

Negotiate. That sounded more positive than 'instantly fired'. But it did still sound as if she might be fighting an uphill battle. Alice was certain that Liam had considerably more negotiating practice than she did.

She'd never liked conflict, a legacy from her peacemaker mother, she'd always thought. Mum had been an expert at smoothing over any situation, defusing every fight, and Alice had picked the habit up from her. It had served her well with her friends in her teenage years, and her housemates at university and in her early twenties.

But in her marriage the skill had evolved into appeasement. Into making herself smaller so there was less to fight about. She'd given up on things she'd believed in, just to avoid an argument. Stopped having her own opinions, her own thoughts. Even stopped fighting her own corner.

Until the day the fights stopped being angry words and slammed doors, and became something more.

The minute she'd woken up in that hospital, her whole life changed for ever, she'd promised herself she'd never give in and play nice, just to avoid a fight, ever again.

So if Liam wanted to negotiate, she would damn well negotiate harder than any businessman he'd ever had to deal with. Because she was fighting for what mattered to her—the well-being of the women who called Thornwood

Castle their place. The castle might be Liam's home, but it was their refuge. Their safe haven.

And that mattered more to Alice than anything else had since that hospital bed.

That, she would fight for.

Placing her cutlery in the finished position, Alice pushed her empty plate away from her and rested her hands in her lap as she waited for Liam to finish eating too, watching him shovel food into his mouth, the action totally incongruous with his dinner jacket and bow tie. Consciously, she straightened her back, lowered her shoulders and practised the calming breathing that one of the courses from earlier in the year had taught her. Liam, apparently unaware that he'd just gained his fiercest opponent yet, continued eating.

Since he wasn't paying her any attention anyway, Alice allowed herself a moment to study him. He was more attractive than she'd expected, she admitted to herself. His photo on his website showed his face half in shadow—a professional headshot in black and white, with a sombre expression and a tie knotted tightly around his neck. In person, seeing him every day, he wasn't like that at all. He seemed relaxed, at home and untroubled by life—even in black tie.

Alice frowned as she realised how unlikely that was.

She didn't know the whole of Liam's story, but for him to be Rose's only living relative, well, that kind of hinted that there wasn't a lot of family in his life. In fact, she knew more than that—Rose had told her once that he'd been orphaned young. Add in the whole 'his father never acknowledged him before he died' thing, which *everyone* knew about, and, well... Untroubled by life and Liam Jenkins probably didn't go together in a sentence often, did they?

But she wouldn't have guessed that from looking at him.

Liam shoved his last forkful of Maud's leftover roast into his mouth, moaned appreciatively as he chewed, and closed his eyes as he swallowed.

'*That* is a hell of a lot better than those fiddly canapés.'

Alice allowed herself a small smile. He liked the food—that much had been clear from the way he hadn't missed a meal in the dining hall since he'd arrived. That in itself was a start—and not always a given with visitors from overseas. Maud had strong feelings about the sort of meals that should be served in a British castle. If a person wasn't into roasted meats, goose fat roast potatoes and a whole lot of gravy, there wasn't much for them in Maud's kitchen. But Liam had been vocally appreciative of her meals, which had definitely earned Maud's approval.

'I'm glad you enjoyed it,' Alice said.

Liam put down his cutlery and opened his eyes, his dark blue gaze meeting hers across the table. 'But now it's time to talk.'

'Apparently so.' Alice folded her hands in front of her and steeled herself. 'So, you've seen what we do here, I've talked about why it's so important, you've spoken with everyone here tonight about it too. I know you've spent the week getting to know the place. So, now it's your turn. What do you have planned for Thornwood?'

CHAPTER FIVE

LIAM TRIED TO shift mentally from taste bud bliss to business. For some reason, it was more difficult than usual—perhaps because of Alice's nervous gaze on the other side of the table. She was clenching her hands together so tightly that the knuckles were white, and the tension in her shoulders made her look as if she was wearing some sort of torture device to keep her upright—like those ridiculous corsets they all wore in the period dramas.

Liam frowned. Seriously, how many of those things had he watched that he remembered all the details? Apparently the universe had been preparing him to inherit Thornwood all along.

Even if nobody else had.

And, anyway, she wasn't wearing anything of the sort. She was wearing that slippery golden dress that moved with every breath she took, emphasising the cowl neckline that led down to the gentle curve of her cleavage...

Actually, maybe it was the dress that was distracting him. Or Alice in it.

But this wasn't the time for thoughts like that. It was time to lay it all out on the table, and see how Alice took the news.

Reaching up, he loosened his bow tie and left it hanging around his neck, popping open the top couple of buttons of his shirt.

'Okay, well, first off you have to understand that I've had no contact with Thornwood for years. I had no idea of the work you were doing here until I arrived last week, and all I know about it is what I've seen and what you've told me. Understood?'

Alice nodded.

'Good. Then you'll appreciate that when I first learned I'd be inheriting the castle I had my own ideas and plans for the place.'

'Plans that didn't involve helping local women, I'd guess,' Alice said.

'Exactly.'

'But now you've seen what we're doing here, how much good we're doing—'

Liam winced, and she cut herself off without him having to do it for her, which he appreciated. Someone who could read the conversational cues was always easier to reason with.

'My plans...they're already underway,' he admitted. 'I have investors interested, contractors coming out to look at the place next week...' He'd given himself a week to settle in before the first of the appointments his assistant had set up, but now that week was up.

'So finding us here has put a real spanner in the works.'

'You could say that.'

Alice bit her lower lip, and Liam hoped against hope that she wasn't about to start crying. He never knew what to do with crying women.

Well, he did. But those women weren't Alice Walters. They weren't his great-aunt's employee, or the woman he was about to turf out of her home. Liam was pretty sure his usual methods of cheering up women wouldn't work so well on Alice right now. Or ever, possibly.

'So. You're going to make us leave.' Alice's expression grew mulish and Liam knew that, even if that was what he'd planned, it wouldn't be as easy as the words suggested. He might own the castle, he might have all the money and the power in this situation, but Alice, doing what she believed in, was a force to be reckoned with.

In that sense, she almost reminded him of his great-aunt Rose.

'I didn't say that,' he pointed out.

'But that's what it comes down to, isn't it?' Alice snapped back. 'The women and families we're helping here aren't as important as whatever money-making scheme you've got ready to go.'

'Hey.' Liam put some edge in his voice, a sharpness clear enough to make Alice settle back down in her seat, at least. 'I understand your frustration—'

'Frustration!' Alice cried, and he gave her a look.

'But that doesn't mean I'm going to let you yell and rant at me before you've actually heard my proposal.'

'Let me? Ha. What on earth makes you think that a man like you *lets* me do anything?' Alice pushed her chair away from the table and stood, hands planted firmly on the wood between them. Liam waited patiently for her to catch on. 'Listen to me, mister. My life is entirely my own. Nothing you do, say or want can influence it without my say-so. This might be your castle, but that doesn't mean that I'm part of the property, okay? You don't *let me* do—' She broke off suddenly, and Liam knew her ears were catching up with her mouth at last. 'Your proposal?'

'Yes, my proposal.' Liam rolled his eyes. 'Why don't you take a seat and we can discuss it? Rationally. Without either of us trying to make the other do anything they don't want to do. Okay?'

Alice's eyes were cautious, but she lowered herself back into her chair all the same. 'I doubt we can manage that,' she said, most of the anger gone now. 'I mean, the very fact that you're calling it a proposal, and that you talked about negotiations before, suggests that your plan means that my plans will have to change. And I don't want that.'

'What if I could give you a better plan?'

'A better plan?' Alice scoffed. 'You've been here, what? A week? And you really think you know better than I do what we need here?'

'I think I can offer you something that you wouldn't have considered an option before.' He'd given this a lot of thought, while he'd been exploring the estate. Alice really was doing good work at Thornwood. And, given his own history, he couldn't just cast that aside. He just needed her to do it in a way that worked for him.

'Which is?' Alice asked, her tone sceptical.

'A dedicated building, for you to run the services you're already running here.'

Alice narrowed her eyes at him. 'What's the catch?'

'No catch,' Liam said with a shrug. 'I admire the work you're doing here. I think hiring you might have been Rose's last-ditch attempt to get into heaven, but that doesn't mean it was a bad idea. So I want you to continue.'

'Just not at Thornwood Castle.'

'Right.'

Alice leant back in her chair, still eyeing him suspiciously. 'So, let me check I've got this straight. You're going to turf us out of the castle into some other outbuilding on the estate, probably without heating or running water, and let us muddle through as best we can until we give up and leave you alone with your castle and your plans.'

Liam took a deep breath and tried to sound patient. 'No. I'm going to relocate you and your groups to a suitable building somewhere else on the estate. I'll also continue to pay your salary and give you an agreed amount of funding for your work every month.'

'There are no suitable buildings on the estate,' she said, wilfully ignoring his generous financial offer.

'I don't *have* to keep you here, you realise. There's nothing in the will about it.' At least, as far as he knew. He hadn't *actually* got all the final details yet. But if he could get Alice to agree to his terms he was pretty sure they wouldn't matter anyway.

'Then why are you?' Always so suspicious.

'Because you're right—you are doing good work here. And I respect that. I… My mother and I had to run to a women's refuge once. We left in the middle of the night, taking nothing with us. We had no money, no support, nothing—and they helped us. If we'd had somewhere like Thornwood, maybe we'd have been able to prepare better, or get out sooner, before it got so…bad. But regardless, I'm not about to kick all the women you help out into the street.'

'And that's very laudable,' Alice said, a hint of sarcasm in her voice. 'But it doesn't change the fact that there are no suitable buildings on the estate. So there's nowhere for you to move us to.'

'Nothing at all?' Liam raised his eyebrows. 'I find that hard to believe on an estate this size.' In fact, he knew different. He'd found at least six possible sites on just one afternoon's walk around the grounds.

Alice waved a hand, dismissing his objections. 'Just some broken-down old barns and the odd decrepit cottage.'

Liam settled back with a satisfied smile spreading on his lips. 'There you go, then.'

'You're going to throw these women out into draughty, falling-down buildings more suitable for housing animals?' The outrage on her face was almost comical. Liam resisted the urge to laugh at her, purely because he needed her on his side.

Which meant explaining. He hated explaining himself.

'Did you, at any point after you discovered that I would be inheriting Thornwood Castle, do any research into me and, say, my career?'

Alice blinked, the anger fading from her expression in the instant her eyes were closed. 'You plan to renovate a barn for us to use?'

Huh. Less explanation required than he'd expected. That was a good sign. Someone who could follow his train of thought without him having to sound out every single syllable was someone he might just be able to work with.

'If that turns out to be the best option, yes.' Pushing his chair away from the table, Liam got to his feet and paced the length of the table. He always thought better on his feet and, to be honest, he hadn't had the time to think the details of his idea all the way through just yet. 'I'm going to be having a lot of work done around the estate anyway, so adding one more building won't affect anything too much. I'm sure you have ideas about exactly what you require—' He glanced at Alice for agreement and she nodded firmly. 'So we take a look around together, find a suitable place, fix it up and move you in.'

'That easy, huh?' Alice still looked sceptical.

Liam shrugged. 'I don't see why not.' It wasn't as if he hadn't turned around bigger projects in record time. A building for a group of women to meet and knit and talk in…how hard could that be?

* * *

It couldn't be that easy. It never was, in Alice's experience.

'And what, exactly, are you expecting in return?' she asked.

Liam raised his eyebrows, gripping the back of his chair as he looked down at her, his bow tie hanging loose around his neck. He looked like a libertine from the twenties, ready for late-night cocktails, and it was incredibly distracting. Alice resisted the urge to stand up, to make them more equal again. This was a negotiation. She couldn't let him know he had her rattled, or that he'd gained the upper hand in any way. Even if it was just by being unfairly good-looking.

But the truth was, she'd been blindsided. She'd expected to fight for the survival of her women's groups. She'd expected to have to argue for the right to stay, to continue her work. And she'd certainly expected Liam to drive a hard bargain.

Instead, he seemed to be offering her exactly what she needed—a purpose-built building for her groups, perhaps even with proper heating. And so far he hadn't asked for anything in return.

No doubt about it, there had to be a catch.

'In return?' Liam asked. 'I get Thornwood Castle back. What more could I want?'

No, that definitely sounded too innocent. 'That's what I want to know.'

He flashed her a wolfish smile. 'So suspicious.'

'With good reason.' Reasons she didn't plan on sharing with him. 'So why don't you tell me *exactly* what you're planning here at Thornwood?'

'Okay, okay.' Throwing up his hands in defeat, Liam took his seat again. 'What do you want to know?'

'You mentioned building works. Are you planning on

knocking the whole place down and starting again?' It was a joke, mostly. But the more she thought about it, the more nervous the idea made her.

Liam laughed. 'No. Even I have more respect for the old place than that. But I do want to make some changes.'

'Like a roof that doesn't leak? Maybe even some working heating?' Those were the sort of changes Alice could get behind.

'Definitely those. But also some bigger changes to the grounds and accommodation here.'

'Like?'

Liam's expression turned serious again. 'I want to make Thornwood accessible to the wider world for the first time.'

'I'm not exactly keeping people out of here, you realise.' Thornwood had already thrown open its doors. It didn't need whatever grand gesture Liam had planned.

'Yeah. But your people...' He trailed off, and Alice made the leap to the obvious conclusion.

'The women and children I help aren't going to make you rich.' Of course it came down to money. Didn't it always with people like him?

'I want Thornwood to be self-sustaining,' Liam countered. 'And that means it needs to earn money from the people visiting it.'

He made it sound perfectly reasonable, but Alice knew what it meant. 'You mean you're going to turn Thornwood into the sort of tourist attraction your aunt would have hated,' she said bluntly.

'Basically.' Liam smiled unapologetically. 'I kind of imagine my ancestors rolling in their graves.'

'And you like that? That you're disrupting centuries of tradition here, going against what Rose would have wanted?'

Just like that, all of Liam's laid-back charm disappeared.

'Rose didn't want to leave me Thornwood in the first place, so don't pretend that she did. She said she wanted me to make it my home at last. Well, fine. This is what *I* want my home to be.'

'Really?' Somehow Alice found that hard to believe. 'Is that what home is to you? Complete strangers trampling through it all the time, gawking?'

'Isn't that what you've done? Opened my home to strangers?'

'It's different, and you know it,' Alice snapped. She frowned. Something in his words was niggling at the back of her mind, but she couldn't quite put her finger on it.

Liam sighed. 'Look, I'm offering you a good deal here. I'll even let you help choose the location—'

'So generous,' Alice murmured, still running his past sentences through her brain again.

'And we can have you set up somewhere else on the estate early in the spring, if things go well, and whatever renovations we decide on don't require planning permission.'

The spring. Alice looked up sharply. 'That long?'

'It's December, Alice. I'm good, but I'm not a miracle-worker. I'd say we're looking at February at the earliest, and that's only if we can agree on a location quickly— preferably one in decent condition.' He frowned. 'Is that a problem?'

'I just… I hadn't planned on staying that long.' She'd been putting off thinking about it, but she'd already stayed longer at Thornwood than anywhere since she'd left Robert. She'd sworn then that she wouldn't let herself get tied down like that again—wouldn't risk being trapped that way. Thornwood had always seemed a safe place, especially with Rose there, and she'd been doing good work. It had been easy to get sucked into that comfortable, secure feeling again.

But Alice knew that sort of security was only ever an illusion. Liam Jenkins's arrival had only made that clearer.

Maybe it was time to go.

'You hadn't… You're not staying?' Liam's eyebrows rose up in surprise. 'Then why am I working this hard to save a scheme you don't even care enough about to hang around and run?'

'It's not that I don't care,' Alice said, fast. 'I do. Very much. This…what I've set up here, it's important. It's one of the best things I've done in my life.'

'Then why go?'

'It's just…time.' She felt awkward just saying it, letting him see that it mattered to her.

But the way Liam surveyed her across the table, she got the feeling he might just possibly understand.

And then, finally, the words he'd spoken that had been stuck in the back of her mind made their way to the front.

'She said she wanted me to make it my home at last.'

At last.

Which made it sound as if he'd refused to make Thornwood home in the past, while Rose was alive. But why?

If she didn't stick around, she'd never know. And, more importantly, she'd lose any power she had to make sure that Liam continued the work she'd started the way he'd promised—with a new building and plenty of financial support. She couldn't leave until she was sure that the women she was leaving behind were safe.

She forced a smile. 'It's fine. I'm happy to stay—at least until everything here is settled.'

'So you'll move your group to whatever building I find for you?'

Nice try. 'No. So I'll stay and help you find the perfect place for my groups, somewhere even better than Thornwood Castle, and get them settled in. And then I'll leave.'

'The *perfect* place?'

'Well, of course.'

Liam sighed. 'In that case, we'd better get started. In my experience, perfection is pretty hard to come by.'

Alice didn't smile. She knew that better than most people.

She was leaving anyway. If he'd just held out, she might have agreed to leave without the promise of a new venue for her groups. And then he could have...what, exactly? Kicked a load of needy women and children out on the streets? Or, worse, back to abusive homes?

No, he couldn't have done that. He knew too well how it felt to have nowhere to go. Nowhere that felt safe. Nowhere to call home.

And now he had Thornwood. Which felt neither safe nor homely, but at least had the benefit of being potentially lucrative.

Once he'd turfed out the current inhabitants, of course.

Standing, he held a hand out across the table to Alice. 'So, we have a deal?'

She took it, her grip firmer than he expected from her pale face and slender form. 'We do.'

'Good.' He scanned her eyes, looking for any hint of emotion—doubt or fear or anything, but there was nothing there. Nothing at all.

He knew that expression. He'd practised it himself.

What was Alice Walters hiding? He suspected he might never know her full story, but he could guess a little of it right now. This wasn't just a job to Alice; this was personal.

Someone, some time, had put Alice in the same position as some of these women.

The thought made him irrationally angry, and his jaw clenched tight.

'Um, can I have my hand back now?' Alice tilted her head to the side as she asked, obviously surveying him the same way he had her.

He wondered what she saw. Then he decided he probably didn't want to know.

'Of course.' He dropped her hand and stepped back from the table. 'In that case, I'd better get back to work—unless you need my help ushering out the last of your guests? I'm figuring the main event must be over by now.'

Alice nodded. 'I think so. I'll go and check everything went okay with the silent auction, say any last goodbyes, and then I can finally get out of this damn dress and off to bed.'

The dress. Just the mention of it made Liam study it again, taking in those delicate straps, seemingly made out of thin golden rope, holding up the fabric that draped across her body, before widening into a fuller skirt. Something about it hinted at the idea that it might just fall to the floor at any moment.

Liam had to admit, he liked it a lot better than the woolly cardigans she normally hid herself behind.

'It's a great dress,' he told her with feeling. 'You look gorgeous in it.'

Alice's cheeks flushed a light pink. 'Thank you. Rose always said I had to look the part for these things, so she had someone send a few dresses over for me to choose from. This one was my favourite—not least because it has hidden pockets. Well, it *was* my favourite, before I realised how uncomfortable the bra I have to wear with it is.' Her blush turned darker as she said that, and Liam chuckled.

'Trust me, it's worth the discomfort.' Grinning, Liam started back towards the ballroom via the main hall. He was finally starting to get his bearings in the labyrinthine corridors of Thornwood Castle. Soon he wouldn't even need the sketched map he'd taken to keeping in his pocket, and glancing at only when he was sure no one was looking.

'I'm glad you think so,' Alice said, following him down the corridor. 'You don't scrub up half bad yourself, you know.'

'Aussie surfer dude turned English aristocrat, huh?'

Alice laughed. 'Something like that.'

'Glad to know I can pull it off.' Liam frowned as an unexpected noise echoed off the stone walls of the corridor they were walking down. 'Did you hear that?'

Alice's forehead creased too. 'I'm not sure.' She took another turning and suddenly they were back in the main hall again, its oversized Christmas tree looming over the staircase. From beyond the next set of doors, they could hear the dying chatter of the fundraiser, the last few guests still hanging on in there. But that wasn't the noise that had caught Liam's attention.

The sound rang out again and, this time, there was no doubt in Liam's mind what he was hearing. He knew the sound of a baby crying well enough—from the age of ten upwards, it had seemed every foster home he went to had a new baby—one he was expected to help look after. 'Did someone bring their baby with them tonight?'

Except he couldn't see anyone nearby, and the cry had sounded very close.

As if it was in the room with them.

'I don't think...' Alice trailed off as the baby cried again. Then she stepped closer to the tree, taking slow, cautious steps in her long shimmering dress, as if trying not to spook a wild animal.

Liam followed, instinctively staying quiet.

The crying was constant now, and there was no denying where it was coming from.

Alice hitched up her dress and knelt down on the flagstones, reaching under the spread of the pine needles, dislodging a couple of ornaments as she did so. Then she pulled out a basket—not a bassinet or anything, Liam realised. Just a wicker basket, of the sort someone might use to store magazines or whatever.

A wicker basket with a baby lying in it.

CHAPTER SIX

'WHOSE IS IT?' Liam whispered, as the baby gripped hold of Alice's finger and, just for a moment, stopped crying. She stared down into its unfocused eyes and felt her heart tighten in her chest. Gritting her teeth, she held her emotions in check. There was a reason she stayed away from babies.

And that reason meant she had to get this one back to its mum as soon as possible.

'I have no idea,' Alice murmured back. 'But it's very young. Newborn, even.'

She hadn't spent a great deal of time around babies before she came to Thornwood. But since then she'd met children of all ages—from a day old upwards. And this baby looked smaller, younger, fresher than any of them.

Who could have left it there? Who did she know who was even pregnant? Susie Hughes had given birth the week before, and Jessica Groves wasn't even six months yet. And neither of them would have left their child unattended under a Christmas tree, anyway.

Bracing herself, she lifted the baby out of the basket, taking care to keep the blanket tucked around it for warmth. Underneath, it was naked, except for a small cloth. Alice unwrapped it carefully, focusing on the clinical, hard facts—not the emotions coursing through her body as she held the baby close.

'It's a boy.' Not that it mattered. What mattered was the roughly cut and tied umbilical cord. 'Oh, God, Liam. I think he's just been born. Today, I mean.' Maybe even here at Thornwood. Alice swallowed at the thought of some desperate woman giving birth alone in a cold, dark corner of the castle, while they were all partying in the ballroom. And then leaving her son in the main hall, where he was sure to be found.

Who would be desperate enough to do such a thing?

'And abandoned.' Alice could hear the judgement in Liam's tone, but she didn't have time to argue with him. Later, she could explain the choices that some women had to face, and the reality of their world that could make such a dreadful decision necessary. Later, she could cry and hurt for all the feelings this moment had dredged up from where she'd tried to bury them.

For now, she just needed to get help for the baby.

'We need to call the doctor.' She eased herself to her feet, still clutching the baby close to her chest. Liam tucked a hand under her elbow to help her up.

'And the police,' he added, and Alice shook her head.

'No. Not yet. We need to see if we can fix this ourselves, first.' Getting the police involved would make everything official.

'Why? And besides, if you don't, surely the doctor will,' Liam argued.

'Not Dr Helene,' Alice disagreed. 'She's worked with us before.'

'This has happened before?' Liam's eyebrows shot up.

'No. Not this.' But plenty of other stuff. Enough for Alice to know instinctively that this was a desperate, last chance act for someone—not an act of cruelty. She wasn't about to punish a desperate woman—and certainly not before they'd tried to help her.

The baby started to squirm in her arms again, and Alice joggled him a little to try and calm him. Poor thing was probably starving, or in shock or both. Adjusting her grip, she felt in the hidden pocket in the folds of her dress for her phone and pulled it out. Reception at the castle was spotty, but if she could get hold of Heather at least she'd have some help. Someone she could hand the baby to and take a step back, regroup, recover her equilibrium.

'I need to make some calls,' she said again. 'But we can't... I don't want everyone to see him. Could you...?'

'You want me to get rid of the rest of the guests?' Liam guessed.

Alice nodded, relieved. 'I'll take him through to the library. I can call the doctor from there.' And Heather. She'd be able to get together some things to look after him. They'd need clothes, formula milk...everything. She started a mental list, knowing that Heather's well stocked store cupboard would be able to provide. Practicalities. That was what she needed to think about.

'Okay. I'll meet you there.' Liam turned to push the basket back under the tree before he went, then paused. 'Hey, there's something else in here.' Liam crouched over the basket and pulled out a scrap of paper—one of the leaflets that Alice had distributed around the shops and businesses of the local village, inviting women to Thornwood Castle whenever they needed support or aid.

Apparently someone had taken her up on the offer in a fairly major way.

'Is that writing on the back?' Alice squinted at the paper to try and make it out.

Liam flipped it over and started to read. '*"This is Jamie. He needs your help. I'm leaving him to Alice Walters and*

Liam Jenkins. Please take care of him and tell him I'm sorry and I love him." Well. That answers *all* our questions, then.'

'Jamie,' Alice murmured. 'It suits him.' Jamie had settled down into her arms now, perhaps having cried himself to exhaustion—or perhaps because he needed serious medical help. She needed to get the doctor there quickly… 'Wait. She left him to *me*?'

Oh, God, no. She couldn't take responsibility for a baby. Not now. She couldn't even *think* about this now, because if she did…

A paralysing sadness washed over her as the memories broke out of the cage she'd kept them locked in for the last few years. Since she'd woken up in that hospital bed and knew her life would be something new now. Gazing down at the sleeping baby, the depth of everything she'd lost yawned open inside her, a gaping hole at the centre of her being, one that could never be filled. Not now. That chance had been taken away from her.

Except she was holding a baby in her arms. Almost as if…

'To *us*,' Liam clarified, his voice harsh, and Alice blinked as the moment broke. She had to focus. This was an emergency—one she would deal with the same way she dealt with every other crisis that hit the women at Thornwood. With practicality, sensitivity and order.

Emotions she could deal with later. First, she needed to deal with the astonishing request in the note.

'She left him to me *and* you?' Her, she could understand—she'd been looking after the people of this community for over a year and a half, and Jamie's mother wouldn't necessarily know that she had no experience looking after babies. But why Liam?

'Apparently so.' Liam shoved the note in his jacket

pocket, shaking his head. 'God only knows what his mother was thinking—if she was thinking at all. Go on. You get to the library and make the calls. I'll meet you there once I've got rid of everyone else. We'll deal with what on earth this note means then.'

A plan. Good. That was exactly what she needed.

Alice nodded and, adjusting the baby in her arms, set off for the safety of the library as quickly as she could, given her long dress.

Maybe there would even be some books on childcare in there. God knew they were going to need them.

The library was thankfully empty. Alice sank into one of the battered leather wing chairs in the corner, her legs still shaking. She pulled out her phone again, scrolling through until she found Heather's number.

Heather answered on the third ring and, from the background noise, Alice was interrupting the servers and helpers finishing off the canapés in the kitchen. 'I need you in the library. Now. And grab one of the baby bags on your way.' Her voice stayed steady, which Alice was proud of. She could handle this. She had to—for Jamie.

Heather didn't question the order—she knew as well as Alice that sometimes when help was needed there wasn't time to debate. 'I'll be right there.'

Alice's second call was to Dr Helene, who promised to leave for Thornwood immediately too—although she required a little more information. 'I'll bring more supplies,' Helene promised, and Alice let out a tiny sigh of relief.

She needed professionals here. For all that she wanted to help Jamie's mother, she hadn't a clue what she was doing.

Alice took a shuddering breath and admitted the truth to herself—she was totally out of her depth. She'd protected herself from everything she knew she could never have—

could never be—by avoiding everything to do with babies, as far as that was possible in a place like Thornwood, always filled with mothers and children. She'd never learnt how to change a nappy, or how to soothe a child, or how to know a baby needed feeding.

If someone wanted a fundraiser organising, a seminar programme setting up, an escape route for an abused woman, she was their girl. She could fix the leaky toilets on the ground floor, and plug holes in the draughty windows of Thornwood. She could even manage the accounts and feed fifty women on a budget set for half that number.

But she couldn't look after a baby. That was knowledge she simply didn't have—knowledge she'd never sought or needed.

Until now.

The door to the library opened, and Alice tensed until she saw Liam slip through and shut it firmly behind him.

'The doctor is on her way,' she told him. 'And Heather. Both of them with supplies.'

'Good.' Liam eyed the baby with what Alice was sure was annoyance. But then he added, 'Poor little guy will freeze in this castle if we don't get him some warm clothes and some formula pretty soon.'

'They won't be long,' Alice promised, surprised that he cared at all. Perhaps Liam really did have a softer side— one that he'd kept very well hidden since his arrival at Thornwood.

But tonight wasn't a night for dwelling on the mysteries and annoyances of Liam Jenkins. Alice gazed down at Jamie, adjusting the blanket again to keep his tiny hands covered. Whatever deal she'd just struck with Liam, whatever promises she intended to hold him accountable to, she knew that her decision to stay at Thornwood for the time being had just been made a whole lot easier.

It wasn't just her women, her work or her legacy she needed to see settled before she left. She needed to make sure Jamie was safe and well cared for too—however much it broke her heart.

Until Jamie was reunited with his mother, Thornwood was home. Again.

'Could that phone call have been any more cryptic?' Heather burst into the library, a plastic bag dangling from one hand, the other placed firmly on her hip. 'What the hell is going on up here?'

Wasn't that the most appropriate question ever? Liam was still trying to figure that out, twenty minutes after he'd found that damn note.

Not the baby. Finding the baby was fine—a problem to be solved, a situation to be dealt with by passing it on to the appropriate authorities. The baby wasn't to blame for any of this.

But that note…

The moment he'd seen his name there, linked with Alice's, naming them as carers for Jamie, his whole body had frozen. And then, milliseconds later, the need to run had surged through him. Thornwood wasn't his home and he didn't need anything else tying him to it. This wasn't his place, Jamie wasn't his baby and this wasn't the sort of responsibility he had ever intended to sign up for.

Except he had a feeling that Rose might have made it his responsibility the minute she'd named him in her will.

Heather was still waiting for an answer, Liam realised, looking up at her as she stood in the doorway.

'Shut the door,' Liam commanded, and she obeyed before turning her attention to Alice.

Heather's eyes widened as she caught sight of the baby.

'This is Jamie,' Alice said, her voice soft now he was

sleeping. What was she making of all this? Liam couldn't tell. He'd thought he'd seen the same sort of panic he was feeling in her eyes when they'd found Jamie, but now she looked almost…content, holding him. 'We found him under the Christmas tree.'

'As far as I'm aware, Santa doesn't bring babies,' Heather commented. 'That's usually the stork's prerogative. Have you called the police? No, of course you haven't.' She answered her own question with a sigh. 'Well, at least I get why you needed this, now.' She held out the bag and Liam took it from her and peered inside.

'Nappies, clothes, pre-made formula bottles…you guys think of everything. This happen a lot round here, does it?' They were too well set up for this to be a one-off.

'Random babies being left as Christmas presents? No.' Heather glared at him. Liam wasn't sure if it was because he now owned Thornwood, or just because he was male. Probably both. 'But we do occasionally have women arrive with new babies who need our help. And sometimes they're not able to bring much with them.'

The words she wasn't saying echoed through Liam's head all the same, and his jaw tightened at the thought of them. Women who had to run, fast. Women who were terrified for their children, in fear for their own lives. Women who had nowhere to go except Thornwood. Women like his mother.

When he'd offered Alice his deal—a promise of a place to continue her work, outside of the castle—it had been for his own convenience as much as hers. He needed them out of the castle in a way that wouldn't enrage the local populace, and he hadn't been much inclined to rely on the misogynist tendencies of the occupants of Thornwood village to get away with just kicking them out. That kind of thing never played well in the papers—not to mention on the internet.

But now, watching as Alice carefully unwrapped Jamie—waking him and causing him to scream, of course—ready to put a nappy on him and dress him, he knew it wasn't just about convenience any more. He'd seen enough over the last week to convince him that Alice wasn't a gold-digger, she wasn't sent purely to try him. What she did mattered around here—and it mattered to her.

And for some reason that seemed to mean it mattered to him now too.

'You're doing it wrong,' he said, stepping forward without thinking as Alice tried to get the nappy on backwards. He'd thought those things were fairly idiot-proof these days, but he guessed if someone had never done it before it could take a moment to figure out.

Kneeling beside her, he turned the nappy the right way, so the tabs opened to be fastened at the front.

'I'd have got there in a second,' she grumbled.

'I'm sure you would have,' Liam said mildly. 'But since that would have meant another second of this kid wailing, I figured I'd help. What, never changed a nappy before?'

'She always gives them back at that point,' Heather said from behind them, where she was preparing a pre-made bottle. She sounded amused, which was more than Liam could manage. 'In fact, she gives them back when they cry too, normally. Or fuss. Or spit up. Or anything.'

'Yeah, well, I can't exactly give this one back right now, can I?' Alice snapped. Liam watched her as she struggled to get Jamie's tiny feet into a sleepsuit. Maybe she wasn't as calm as he'd thought. Especially if she had no experience of babies. She had to be freaking out as much as he was; she was just hiding it well.

'I can see why you never had kids,' he joked, trying to lighten the mood, but Alice didn't laugh. In fact, she paused, just for a moment, in dressing Jamie. And when she resumed the action, her hands were trembling.

Damn. He'd hit a nerve and he hadn't even been trying.

What was it with Alice and babies? She was clearly out of her depth here, but reluctant to accept his help. Liam suppressed a sigh. Well, she was just going to have to suck it up and let him help her. Not because *she* needed it, but because Jamie did.

As much as he'd wanted to run, fast and far away from Thornwood, the moment he'd seen his name on that note, he already knew he couldn't. Not now. He couldn't just walk away from an abandoned child, any more than Alice could.

His eyes narrowed as he watched Alice wrap Jamie back up in his blanket. Why was that, exactly? Liam knew why an abandoned baby hit his buttons, but which of Alice's was the situation pressing? Or, the thought occurred suddenly, was it something even simpler?

Alice had been so determined to hold on to Jamie until they found his mother, yet she apparently had no patience or interest in them normally. Did she know who the mother was, perhaps, and this was her way of protecting her? It seemed as likely as any other answer.

Which meant Liam would need to keep a very close eye on Alice, and see who she spoke to over the next day or so. He might have some sympathy for a woman in dire straits who felt she had no choice but to abandon her child—but that didn't mean he agreed with it. There were other options—there was *always* another option—and he intended to have strong words with Jamie's mum about them.

As soon as he found out who she was, anyway.

* * *

Of course, the minute she managed to get Jamie's tiny limbs safely enclosed within the sleepsuit Heather had found and rewrapped him in his blanket, Dr Helene came bustling in through the library door and they had to take everything off again for her to check him over.

Alice liked Dr Helene. She had the sort of no-nonsense approach that tended to calm people—including Alice, tonight. But at the same time she was caring, kind—and very understanding of the work they were doing at the castle. Helene had more than once been able to help out with women in dire straits, and she had great connections in the city too, which always came in helpful with relocations.

But tonight she hadn't come alone. Instead she'd brought a woman who Alice had spoken to many times in the course of trying to help the people of Thornwood.

'Hello, Iona,' Alice said before turning to Helene. 'You brought social services?'

'Iona's a friend,' Helene said. 'She can help us. Now, who does this little man belong to?' Helene frowned as she peeled off the blanket and pulled open the poppers on the sleepsuit.

'That's the million-dollar question,' Liam drawled. Helene glanced up at him, then apparently dismissed him as of no importance. Alice hid a smile; it would do his ego some good to be ignored, but she supposed she'd better perform introductions.

'Helene, this is Liam Jenkins—the new owner of Thornwood. And this—' she pointed at the baby '—is Jamie. We found him here, under the Christmas tree, just wrapped in a blanket with this note.' She nodded to Liam and he handed it over.

Helene scanned the note quickly, and her frown grew deeper. 'Well, he certainly looks like a newborn. And apparently the mother wanted him to be your responsibility. Have you fed him yet?'

Alice shook her head. 'We were about to try when you arrived. I was a little concerned about his umbilical cord…'

'It does look a little rough and ready. But actually it's been done safely, as far as I can tell. It does look like he was born very, very recently though.' She pulled her bag closer and took out the necessary supplies to sterilise the cord stump. 'To someone who knew how to cut the cord without the baby bleeding out, but had no idea what to do next.'

'Except abandon him.' Liam was sounding judgemental again. Alice ignored him. Their judgement didn't matter right now. What mattered was Jamie's well-being.

'I can't even think of any regulars here who it could have been,' Alice said.

'I've been making a list of pregnant women who've visited recently,' Heather put in. 'But I can't see it being any of them either.'

'We'll need to follow up with them, all the same,' Iona said, turning to Helene. 'Is there anyone who has been into the surgery recently who could be a candidate?'

Helene shrugged. 'No one obvious, but then you never know what might overtake someone. And, to be honest, if she chose to have the baby here rather than at the hospital, chances are she might not have had any prenatal care at all. She might not even have known that she was pregnant.'

'That really happens?' Liam asked, obviously sceptical. Alice didn't blame him; it sounded so unlikely. How could anyone not know that there was a life growing inside them? She'd known, within a few days. And when that life was gone…she'd known that too. The loss had almost swallowed her up.

'Not often,' Helene admitted. 'But probably more

often than you'd think.' She finished her examination and straightened up. 'Okay. Let's get this little man wrapped up, fed and asleep. Then we can all talk about what happens next.'

'He's okay?' Alice chewed her lip as she wriggled Jamie back into his clothes. He was so tiny, so helpless. The thought of what might have happened if she hadn't come through the main hall just then, if she'd stayed at the fundraiser and hadn't been back that way that evening... No. She couldn't think that way. Someone would always have found him.

It just felt weirdly like fate that it was her.

'Babies are surprisingly hardy,' Helene said. 'You must have found him very soon after he was left. He'd barely had a chance to get cold. And, lucky for him, it looks like the birth must have been straightforward—although I wish I could examine the mother and make sure she's okay too.'

'His mother.' Alice sighed. 'We have to find her.'

'We will,' Heather promised. 'I'm on it.'

'And in the meantime, I assume you don't want to alert the police just yet?' Helene said. Iona raised her eyebrows.

'Not yet.' Alice thought of some poor, desperate woman being led away in handcuffs for making the worst decision she'd ever have to make. 'Give us a chance to put this right first. Find the mother. Figure out what's best for her and for Jamie.'

Helene nodded. 'Okay. I'll come back tomorrow to check on him, but in the meantime...'

'I can take him,' Iona said. 'We have places we can look after him, until the mother comes forward.'

'And what if she doesn't?' Liam asked. 'If we involve the police, they can launch an appeal, right? Ask the mother to own up.'

'They could,' Iona allowed. 'But that's not always the best move.'

'How do you mean?' Alice asked, frowning. She hadn't thought about appeals. She'd just thought about Jamie, and how his mother had wanted her to look after him. About how she knew, deep inside her, that she *must* do that, however much it hurt, so that Jamie was safe.

'Sometimes those appeals can be counter-productive,' Iona explained. 'The mother knows the baby is safe then, and that makes it easier for her to stay hidden. She's more likely to come forward if she doesn't know what has happened to Jamie, so that she can make sure he's okay.'

That made sense, she supposed, although she hated the thought of some poor woman panicking alone, never knowing what happened to her child. How could anyone live like that?

'Which is why it might make sense for Iona to take him,' Helene said.

'No. His mother wanted me to look after Jamie. I'll take care of him.' Was that her voice? Her words? What was she thinking? She knew nothing about looking after babies. Heather was right—she didn't just pass back the crying babies or the vomiting ones. She handed them all back, the first chance she got. Not because she didn't like them, didn't love their new baby smell and their soft skin. But because…

Because it was just too hard. Being so close to something she knew she could never have, not any more.

So why was she putting herself right next to *this* baby, this helpless child who would hopefully be going home to his mother in the next twenty-four hours? This was the worst idea she'd ever had.

And yet she couldn't bring herself to let him go, to trust anyone else to care for Jamie.

'You?' Liam sounded incredulous. 'You couldn't put a nappy on without help.'

'I'll figure it out,' Alice snapped. 'Don't you think I can do it?'

'On your own?' He raised one eyebrow. 'Probably. But why would you want to?'

'Because he doesn't have anybody!' How could he not understand this? 'He needs help so I will help him. That's what I do. And Heather has her own kids to get home to, and everyone else here has enough on their plates, so it comes down to me, okay? So I will do it.'

'Of course you will. But why do you want to do it on your own?' Alice stopped and stared at him. He could not possibly be suggesting what it sounded like he was suggesting.

'Because that's how I do things,' she said slowly, realising as she spoke the words how true that was. And how sad, actually.

'Yeah, but this time I'm right here.' Liam shrugged. 'She left him to both of us to look after, remember? It's not like I can do much around Thornwood until I get our deal underway, so I might as well help you with this. With him.'

'Sounds like that's sorted, then.' Helene picked up her doctor's bag, and Iona nodded.

'I'll come back tomorrow with Helene to see how things are going,' Iona said. 'But in the meantime, try and keep him away from other people as much as you can, to try and draw the mother out.'

'And good luck!' Helene added.

'No, wait,' Alice started to say, but Iona and Helene were already preparing to leave.

'So we have a plan.' Liam flashed that too charming smile at the other women. 'Then, ladies, thank you for your help. But I think we can take it from here.'

CHAPTER SEVEN

OKAY, HE KNEW this was crazy. What was he thinking, offering to help Alice Walters look after a baby? Had he been thinking at all?

Probably not. But he couldn't forget the note in his jacket pocket—the one asking him to take care of Jamie. Given how many times he'd been turned away by people who should have cared for him, how could he do the same to a helpless baby?

Besides, he saw how the tension in Alice's shoulders had lessened, just slightly, and how the lines around her eyes looked less pronounced as she realised she wouldn't be doing this alone. She knew she needed him; that much was clear. She was still gripping the baby close to her chest, as if she was afraid someone might snatch him from her arms at any moment. But she didn't look quite so much as if she was about to bolt out of the door and run for the hills.

Liam understood the impulse—hadn't he thought of doing exactly the same thing? The only thing he still wasn't sure about was, if she'd run, would she have taken Jamie with her or not?

She obviously didn't have much experience with babies, and from what Heather had said she didn't seem particularly interested in them either—until now. Which brought him back to the nagging question at the back of his mind: what was it about Jamie that made her hold on so tight?

If it *was* that she knew who his mother was, staying close and helping her might enable him to find out too. And if not…well, they might not have got off to the best start but Alice clearly needed his help. He wasn't about to abandon her—or Jamie.

He knew how it felt to be abandoned. Unwanted. Cast out or turned away. He couldn't let this baby, born in Liam's own ancestral home, start his life that way.

Thornwood Castle might never have been a home or even a refuge to him, but Alice had made it one for others. And now it could be one for Jamie too.

'How come you know so much about babies, anyway?' Alice asked, sounding sulky as Jamie started to fuss again. 'Or was the nappy thing just a fluke?'

Liam reached out to take Jamie from her. Alice held on for a second, obviously reluctant to give the baby up to him, but finally released him. Supporting Jamie's neck with one hand, Liam held him against his chest, humming a little to help soothe him.

'Not a fluke,' Helene commented as she shrugged on her coat. Heather looked less impressed, Liam realised, but he doubted there was *anything* he could do to impress *her*.

'I had younger siblings,' he said by way of explanation.

Heather frowned. 'I thought you were Rose's *only* living relative.'

'Foster brothers and sisters,' he expanded. 'Various families, but no blood relatives.'

And that was what it all came down to in the end, for Rose. His blood. It might not be pure, but there was enough of her ancestors' DNA pumping through his body to be better than nothing.

'You were fostered?' Alice asked, her brow furrowed. 'But why—?' Jamie cut her off with a short cry.

'Do you have that bottle?' Liam asked, glad for the interruption. 'I think he's hungry.' Alice gave a quick nod and rooted through the bag, pulling out the sterile bottle, snapping off the lid and screwing on the teat before handing it to him.

Liam slipped the teat between Jamie's lips and waited for the tiny boy to suck. This, he could do. Taking care of a baby might prove easy compared to avoiding Alice's questions, longer term. He might not have known her long, but he was already sure that she was the sort of person who needed all the information, and didn't stop asking questions until she had it.

He knew what she'd been about to ask—why hadn't he come to live with Rose? Given how much respect she'd obviously had for his great-aunt, he suspected the real answer would disappoint her. In fact, she'd probably just assume that he'd refused or done something awful to make Rose reject him.

Which was fine by him. Better than having the world know the truth—that his own family had disowned him, just because his mother wasn't married to his father.

That was all in the past, now. Thornwood Castle was his, and there was no family still alive to look down on him.

Jamie spluttered and he removed the bottle, hardly even surprised when the baby spit up milk across the arm of his shirt.

He was his own man. And he wouldn't turn away a defenceless child the way his family had. Even one that had just thrown up all over his best dinner jacket.

'Well, since you have everything under control here, we'll see you all in the morning,' Helene said. 'And I'll do some digging tonight, see if I can find any leads to Jamie's mum.'

'Me too,' Iona added.

'Heather, are you okay locking up for the night?' Alice was normally responsible for clearing out all the rooms, making sure that doors were closed and locked, in a desperate attempt to keep what little heat the castle had inside. But tonight she had bigger priorities—and she wasn't leaving Jamie alone with Liam. Not because she didn't trust Liam with the baby—from the way he was cradling him as he fed him, she instinctively knew that Liam would take good care of him. But just because...

Did she have to have a reason? Because if she did, she didn't want to analyse it too closely.

'I'll be fine.' Heather shot her an unreadable look. 'Will you?'

Alice glanced away. She hadn't shared much of her past with her friend—or with anyone at Thornwood—but she'd obviously picked up on a few things. Heather might pretend to be brusque and uncaring, but underneath her tough exterior Alice knew she had more feelings than most people. She just hid them better—the result of a lifetime of protecting herself and her kids, Alice supposed.

'I'll be fine,' Alice lied as she took Jamie back from Liam's arms. 'Don't worry.'

She was worrying enough for both of them.

Heather watched her for a moment longer. And then she nodded.

'Okay. Helene? Iona? I'll show you out. Alice, there's a spare travel cot in the cupboard off the library, I think. I'm sure a famous architect will be able to figure out how to set it up.'

And then, with the swing of the door, she was alone with Jamie.

Well, Jamie and Liam.

'I don't need your help,' she told Liam over Jamie's sleeping head.

He smiled infuriatingly. 'Yes, you do.'

'I have books. And the Internet. I can figure this out.'

'Which brings me back to why would you want to? Trust me, babies are always easier when you can tag team. And, besides, you don't know how long it's going to take to find his mother.'

'No. I suppose.' She was out there somewhere, though. Alone, perhaps. And thinking about her son, she was almost certain.

'So we'll do it between us,' Liam said. 'It'll be good practice in working together.'

'Ready for kicking me out of Thornwood?'

'For finding your perfect place.'

Alice held Jamie closer against her chest as Liam picked up the bags of supplies. 'First we need to find that travel cot. And somewhere to put it up.' She hadn't thought that far ahead. There wasn't room in her tiny box bedroom for a travel cot—or any of the other junk babies seemed to come with, if the bags Heather and Helene had left were any indication.

Liam shrugged. 'That part's easy. We'll set it up in Rose's suite. There's plenty of room up there and we can both sleep near enough to hear his every movement, if that's what you're worried about.'

'Rose's suite. You mean your room.' His bedroom, where he slept every night, in his bed.

Alice knew what he was doing. He was taking control of this whole situation, because that was what he did. What he was used to. He'd marched into Thornwood Castle and taken over—holding court during her career sessions, sticking his nose in everywhere, deciding not just the future of the castle but *her* future, and the future of all the women she helped. He had taken charge of every single thing that happened at Thornwood since he'd arrived.

Well, not this time. Not Jamie.

'It's the bedroom that's best equipped to look after a baby in.' Liam gave her that look that suggested he thought she was infuriatingly slow. 'It has the best heating, and there's a daybed in the lounge area as well as the king-sized bed in the bedroom. There's even a mini fridge if we need it, and plenty of empty drawers for Jamie's stuff. It makes sense.'

It makes sense. How many times had she heard that from her husband? Every time she had a suggestion, or a request to do things differently—anything he didn't agree with—he'd put forward his argument instead, always finishing with 'it makes sense'. Dismissing her ideas, her dreams, with just those three words.

Frustration bubbled up inside her just hearing them again. And the very worst part was, this time, Liam was right. It *did* make sense. She just didn't want it to.

'I could set up a camp bed in the library,' she countered. 'It's close to the kitchens, and there's plenty of space.'

'And lots of reading material,' Liam drawled. 'But if there's only one camp bed, where am I going to sleep?'

'In your room. Alone,' she added, in case there was any confusion.

Jamie shifted in her arms, and she took the opportunity to change position. For such a tiny little thing he was getting kind of heavy.

'Then how will I help you?'

'As I said, I don't need your help.'

'You say that now. But at two in the morning, when he's been screaming for an hour or two, you'll be knocking on my door begging for help.'

'No. I won't.' She sounded like a stubborn toddler and

she didn't care. Jamie was her responsibility, whatever that note said, and she would take care of him. Somehow.

Liam sighed. 'No, you probably won't. And that's the problem.'

'Why is that a problem? I thought a self-described care-free, fun-loving bachelor would appreciate a full night's sleep. All the better to get on with his carefree, fun-loving ways.' Nobody in their right mind would describe Liam Jenkins as the responsible, paternal type. At least, no one who'd met him.

'I have *never* used those words to describe myself,' Liam said, sounding amused. 'And I want to because if you spend all night dealing with him then you'll be a wreck tomorrow. Share the load a little and you might be able to function in the morning. I don't imagine life at Thornwood Castle will halt just because you took in a waif and stray.'

Damn him, but he had a point. She had three classes planned tomorrow.

'Plus if the mother shows up, you want to be awake enough to talk with her,' he added, and Alice gave up the argument.

Well, part of it, anyway.

'Fine. We'll set the travel cot up in the lounge area, and I'll sleep on the daybed. You keep to your usual bed, and I'll be able to call you if I need you.'

For a moment Liam looked like he was about to argue, but in the end he gave a sharp nod. 'Fine. I'm a light sleeper. I'll leave the door open, so I'll hear him anyway.'

Alice shrugged. 'Your choice.'

'A compromise.' Liam's mouth twitched up into a lop-sided smile. 'Look at us. Finding a way to compromise. That bodes well for the future.'

'That or it's a sign of the apocalypse.' Alice nudged Jamie's head into a more comfortable position. 'Come on. Let's get this cot set up. This boy is getting heavy.'

The travel cot had been designed by a masochist, Liam decided. Who else would make it so damn difficult for sleep-deprived new parents to set up somewhere for their baby to sleep? He'd had a full eight hours last night, was only temporarily performing parental duties and had several advanced qualifications in architecture and engineering, and he still couldn't do it.

No. He *would* do it. It was just taking a little longer than he'd hoped.

'Are you still trying to get that thing set up?'

Of course, Alice's running commentary was *definitely* helping.

'Whoever designed this hates me,' he said, shoving one side down to try and get it to click into place. 'Like, they have a personal vendetta and they hate me passionately. It's the only explanation.'

Alice gave out a small squeak, and when he looked back over his shoulder he saw her lips were pressed together tightly as if she were trying not to laugh.

'Here, take Jamie.' She held the baby out to him. 'Let me have a go.'

'This is trickier than nappies, trust me,' Liam said, but he took Jamie all the same. Let her try. She was always so convinced that she could do everything herself, and better than anyone else—let her have a go.

Alice pulled a piece of paper from the bag the travel cot had been packed in, scanned it quickly, then did something he couldn't quite follow with one of the sides of the cot. Then she reached inside, pressed something, and stood back.

'All done. Where's the mattress?'

Liam nodded towards the pile of stuff Heather and Helene had left for them, amazed. Alice retrieved the mattress, settled it in place, then stretched a sheet across it.

'He'll probably refuse to sleep in it anyway. Don't you have a bassinet or something around here?' It wasn't that he was feeling emasculated or anything. Just annoyed that he couldn't work the bloody thing.

And even more annoyed that she could.

'This is the best we have for now.' Alice went back to rifling through the bags and pulled out a book from one of the bags the doctor had left. 'I'll try and get hold of a pram tomorrow. And, actually...' she reached deeper and pulled out a large swathe of swirly purple and blue material '...Helene left us a sling. So at least we can try carrying him in that until then.'

'Are there instructions?' Liam squinted at the sling. 'Because that looks more confusing than the travel cot.'

Alice smiled across the room at him, then covered her mouth as her smile turned into a yawn. 'We'll figure it out tomorrow. It's late, and it's already been a long day.'

Liam suspected that the night would be even longer, but it didn't seem worth reminding Alice of that right now. Jamie had been as good as gold so far, only squawking when he needed food or changing, but Liam had spent enough nights trying to sleep through babies crying to know that the chances were good it wouldn't last past their heads hitting the pillow.

Although maybe that was just the babies his various foster parents had taken in. The ones who had already been abandoned, left with adults who were only looking after them for the cash.

Liam knew there were good foster parents out there—wonderful people who took children in to give them a better life, a better start. He'd met plenty of them since he'd grown up, mostly through his charitable work with foster carers in the past decade. Once he'd found his feet, and his success, he'd wanted to give back—not to the system that had failed him, exactly, but to the other kids who ended up in his position. He wanted to make their chances a little better, their futures a little brighter.

So yeah, he knew there were great foster parents out there. He just hadn't had the good fortune to be fostered by any of them.

And now Jamie… He'd been abandoned too, left behind too. And all he had was Liam and Alice.

He hoped they could do a better job than the people who'd pretended to look after him over the years of his childhood.

'Are you okay with him for a few moments? Just while I go and get my overnight stuff?' Alice bit her lip as she waited for his answer, and she looked so uncertain, so concerned for Jamie, that for a moment Liam forgot to feel offended by her lack of confidence in him and just enjoyed knowing that this abandoned child, at least, would be loved.

He didn't know what Alice's issues were, what secrets she was hiding. But he knew that she loved Jamie already. He was barely half a day old, had no blood connection to Alice, and they didn't even *know* who his parents were, let alone care. But Alice loved that baby.

And that made her a good person. He could compromise for a good person. He could help her out.

Liam smiled and held Jamie a little closer. 'I'll be fine.'

'Okay, then.' Alice's blonde head disappeared through the door, and Liam let out a sigh of relief. He wasn't used to sharing space, yet here he was inviting a woman he barely knew and a baby he'd just met into his bedroom.

Well. He'd known that coming home to Thornwood would change his life.

Jamie wriggled in his arms and let out a small mewling cry.

'Shh… Shh…' Liam murmured, pressing a kiss to the top of the baby's head. 'It's all fine. Everything is fine. I'm here.'

Apparently Jamie didn't find that very reassuring, as his cries grew louder. Liam paced the room, jostling Jamie gently as he walked. Time to bring out the big guns.

Taking a deep breath, Liam began to hum, gratified as the music started to calm the baby. Growing in confidence, he opened his mouth and started to sing—snatches of lullabies and nursery rhymes he half remembered, interspersed with other songs from his childhood.

Jamie blinked up at him, silent again, and Liam couldn't help but smile down at his innocent face.

'It's all going to be fine, Jamie,' he whispered. 'I promise you. I'll make sure that everything is okay for you. I don't know how, but I will. You're never going to have to worry about being abandoned again.' He shouldn't promise anything, he knew. He wasn't staying at Thornwood. He had no power over Jamie's future. But, although the little boy didn't understand him, Liam couldn't bear the thought of Jamie feeling unwanted or lost for even a moment. 'You'll have a home. And a family. Somehow. I'll make it happen.'

Jamie would never grow up the way he had. He wouldn't allow it.

CHAPTER EIGHT

ALICE PAUSED IN the doorway, watching Liam pacing up and down the lounge area of the suite, Jamie nestled in his arms. He was talking to the baby, she realised, and strained closer to hear the words without being spotted.

'You'll have a home. And a family. Somehow. I'll make it happen.'

Her chest tightened at Liam's words. What had happened to make him so attached to a tiny baby on just a couple of hours' acquaintance? She knew it had to be connected with the baby being abandoned—his reaction to that had made his feelings very clear.

What she didn't know was what demons in Liam's past made him feel it so deeply. And what she didn't understand was why she cared.

Liam Jenkins had arrived at Thornwood ready to toss her out on her ear, along with all the other women she helped there. But instead he'd listened—maybe not immediately, but soon enough—and he'd changed his mind. He'd engaged with the work. He'd recognised its importance.

He might still be kicking her out, but at least he was making sure she had somewhere to go first. And now it looked as if he was doing the same for Jamie.

Liam looked up and caught sight of her in the doorway.

Holding up her overnight bag, Alice tried to make it look like she'd just arrived.

'How's he doing?' she asked.

'Just dozed off again. Might be a good time to try and put him down.'

Alice dumped her bag by the sofa and tried to remember what Helene's book had said. 'Don't we need to feed and change him first?'

Liam shrugged. 'He'll wake up when he's hungry or wet.'

'But won't he sleep longer if we do it now?' From the little she'd read and heard, maximising sleep was an important part of looking after babies. 'Plus, shouldn't we be trying to get him into a routine?'

She should be telling, not asking, she realised. She'd wanted to take control of this situation, but here she was, in his room, asking his advice.

On the other hand, he was the only one of them that had any idea about looking after babies. So maybe she was just being prudent.

'Stop overthinking it,' Liam advised. 'Chances are we'll find the mother tomorrow, get him home where he belongs—or find him a better place to be. But he won't—'

'He won't be here. Right.' Because he wasn't her son, this wasn't her life. Jamie would go to a new home, new parents, and they'd take care of getting him into a routine, and making sure he was taking the right amount of formula every few hours.

Someone else would be holding him, and putting him down to sleep. Which was just as it should be.

She really had to remember that.

'Put a blanket in the cot?' Liam asked. Alice blinked and jumped to do it, smoothing out the waffle blanket over the sheet.

Liam laid Jamie on top of the blanket, his head sticking out the top, then wrapped the blanket securely around his body.

'Swaddling?' Alice asked, surprised.

'Hardly,' Liam scoffed. 'Just keeping him warmly wrapped. My memory of childcare isn't good enough to remember the official way to do it.'

'He looks happy enough.'

Alice stood beside Liam and they gazed down at the sleeping baby.

It shouldn't feel so right, Alice knew. She shouldn't let herself feel so attached.

And yet she couldn't help it.

'You should take the bed,' Liam murmured. 'I'll be fine on the daybed.'

'A gentlemanly gesture?' Alice asked, surprised. 'Not likely. I want to be in here with Jamie.'

Liam sighed. 'Fine. It won't matter anyway. It's not like either of us are going to be getting much sleep.'

'Probably not,' Alice agreed. Normally, a bad night's sleep would bother her. But right then, looking down at Jamie sleeping peacefully…she didn't care at all.

She just wanted to see Jamie's blue eyes when he opened them again.

Sadly, Liam's words proved prophetic. No sooner had he managed to fall asleep—which wasn't as easy as it sounded—than he heard Jamie wake for the first time.

Resting an arm across his tired eyes, he waited to see if the baby might settle again. He'd already lain there awake for hours, listening to the small sounds from the next room. He wasn't used to sharing his space, and something about knowing Alice was just an open door away was distracting. Not to mention Jamie. Alice was the one lying beside the baby, listening for every breath, he was sure, but Liam couldn't help but try to do the same. What if something happened to him during the night? What if Alice didn't know how to deal with it?

God only knew how real parents coped with that kind of fear, night after night. It was driving him crazy and the baby was technically nothing to do with him.

Except for how it was living in his house. And sleeping next door. With his…employee? Lodger? Squatter? How exactly was he supposed to describe his relationship with Alice—especially now they appeared to be co-parenting a foundling child?

Jamie cried out again, and Liam decided to leave the ruminations for a more reasonable hour of the morning. Shoving the covers aside, he rolled out of bed, padding across the floor to the doorway.

Alice had turned on a small lamp in the corner of the lounge, and her hair glowed honey-gold in the soft light. She was bent over the crib, shushing Jamie as she stroked his head.

'Is he hungry?' Liam whispered, crossing to where she stood.

Alice shook her head. 'I don't think so. His eyes aren't even open; I'm not sure he's fully awake.'

Sure enough, after a few more moments, Jamie stilled again and his breathing evened out.

'You didn't have to get up,' Alice said, turning away.

'I know.' He could have waited, let Alice deal with it. But somehow he'd wanted to be there too.

Alice looked up at him, strangely vulnerable in the low light. For a moment, just a brief flash of a second, Liam could almost believe that this was real. That this was his life. His home, his family, his…Alice.

But it wasn't, not really.

He looked away. 'We should get some more sleep.'

Alice yawned in response.

Jamie woke a few more times in the night, usually settling again after milk or a nappy change. After the first couple, Liam left Alice to it—she only glared when he went in, anyway. But around three in the morning, Jamie started crying and didn't stop.

He gave it fifteen minutes, then went in to take over.

'My turn,' he said, holding his arms out for the baby.

Alice gave him the same glare he'd been getting all night, never stopping bouncing Jamie in her arms. 'I can do this.'

'You've *been* doing this all night. Now it's my turn.'

'Because you don't think I can do this.'

'Because you need a break.' He rolled his eyes. 'Just accept the help. Hand him over and go back to sleep.'

It took her thirty seconds or so to finally decide in his favour, and he could almost hear the argument she was having with herself in her brain. Then she yawned and handed him the baby.

'His bottles and nappies and everything are over there.' She waved a hand vaguely in the direction of the pile of stuff she'd piled up in the corner, and stumbled towards the daybed.

'Use my bed,' Liam said, and Alice paused. But obviously tiredness had begun to catch up with her, because she gave a small nod and changed her trajectory towards the bedroom.

Liam gave her a few seconds to reach the bed, then firmly shut the door behind her.

'Just you and me now, kid,' he told Jamie, who blinked in response.

How hard could this be?

* * *

Jamie's wails echoed off the lonely stone walls of Thorn-wood Castle. Liam kept pacing. He was far enough away on the ground floor that he was pretty sure Alice couldn't hear him, which was the most important thing. She needed her sleep—if only so he could go back to bed without guilt when she got up and took over again.

For all his assurances that he knew what he was doing, Liam was starting to doubt himself. He jostled Jamie against his shoulder again, as the baby seemed to prefer being upright to lying down, and rubbed his palm against his lower back. Jamie's cries snuffled and stopped, and Liam held his breath, not even wanting to look to see if his eyes were closed. Maybe, maybe…

Jamie let out another long, desolate cry, and Liam let out the breath he'd been holding.

'Not tired yet, huh?' he murmured.

Maybe he needed those childcare books Alice had been talking about, he thought, as his pacing led him towards the library. God knew he'd done everything he could think of.

Jamie had a dry nappy on, he'd drunk plenty of milk and declined the last bottle Liam had offered him, and he was warm and cosy—but not too hot. After that, Liam was out of ideas.

'Let's go see if we can find you a story,' Liam suggested without much hope. Obviously Jamie was far too young to understand books and stories, but maybe the sound of him reading to him would soothe him. It was worth a try, anyway.

Liam found a stack of picture books on a low shelf by the library door and picked a few at random, settling into a leather wingback chair with Jamie nestled in the crook of his arm. Once again, Jamie's cries lessened for a moment, but soon he was drowning out the words of the nursery rhyme book Liam had chosen.

Liam sighed. 'Be honest. Is this punishment for something I did in another life? Or are you just bored?'

Jamie's only response was to cry louder.

Exhausted, Liam let his head fall back against the chair and his eyes close. What on earth had he been thinking, agreeing to this—no, insisting on this? He wasn't meant to be playing happy families with a woman who didn't trust him and a baby that had landed unceremoniously underneath their Christmas tree. And he wasn't meant to be settling in at Thornwood either—he was supposed to be shaking things up and changing everything.

But instead he was spending all his energies on a tiny scrap of humanity who *would not stop crying.*

'I must have been mad,' he whispered. 'Actually crazy to even come back here.' Hadn't he known that Thornwood was the worst place for him to be? A place where he could never belong, and where he would always, always be found wanting?

Jamie was just bringing that home to him in a very vocal way. He couldn't do this, and he shouldn't even have wanted to try. This wasn't his life.

Jamie gave a tiny hiccup, mid cry, and the strange sensation seemed to be enough to quiet him for a moment. Liam opened his eyes and looked down into unblinking blue ones, and knew in an instant that none of it mattered.

Yes, he didn't belong here. Yes, he probably couldn't do this. And yes, this wasn't at all how he'd pictured his time at Thornwood going.

But he was going to do it anyway.

Because this tiny child, less than a day old, needed him. And that made him his responsibility, regardless of blood ties or his mother's request. Jamie *needed* him, and that was enough. More than enough.

Liam couldn't walk away now if he wanted to.

Jamie's little face started to screw up again, and Liam eased himself to his feet with a groan.

'Come on, little man. If you're going to be staying here, you need to get to know the place. Let's have a tour. We can start with Rusty—that's Alice's favourite suit of armour, you know.' He held Jamie a little closer, and breathed in the scent of him. 'You and me, we can get to know this place together. Okay?'

Because, however hard it got, Jamie was his responsibility now, for as long as the little boy needed him. And Liam wasn't going to let him down.

Where was she?

Alice sat bolt upright in a bed that definitely wasn't hers—it was far too comfortable. She blinked into the darkness for a few moments before the events of the previous night came flooding back.

She was in *Liam's* bed. Because they were looking after a baby together. And she'd spent half the night staring fixedly at the cot where Jamie was sleeping just in case he stopped breathing, until Liam had taken over and told her to get some sleep…

Jumping out of the bed, she raced for the door and yanked it open.

The lounge was empty.

Logically, she knew that Liam wouldn't have taken Jamie far—they were in his home, for heaven's sake—but that didn't make her heart pound any less. Pausing only to grab her slippers—the stone floors were freezing—she dashed out of Liam's suite and headed for the stairs, listening all the while for the sound of a baby's cries.

She heard nothing.

Nothing as she passed the Christmas tree where they'd found him, nothing as she ran past the library. Nothing at all...until she neared the kitchen.

The smell of bacon cooking was unmistakable, but it was far too early for Maud to have arrived. And Maud didn't sing songs from the musicals in a light tenor.

Alice slowed, smiling, as she took the steps down to the kitchen.

Inside, she saw Liam at the stove, turning bacon as he sang, while Jamie lay on a blanket, surrounded by cushions, on the floor a few feet away.

'Ready for breakfast?' he asked without turning, and she wondered how he knew she was there.

'You said you weren't going to take him anywhere.'

'You said,' Liam corrected her. 'And I didn't. We're still in the castle.'

'I meant stay in the suite.'

'He got bored, and I didn't want him to wake you up. So I took him on a little tour of the castle, introduced him to Rusty outside your office, and now we're raiding Maud's supplies to make you breakfast.'

'That's...kind of you.' She crossed to where Jamie was staring into the middle distance and knelt beside him to hide her confusion.

She wasn't sure what she'd expected when Liam had offered to help her out with Jamie, but breakfast hadn't really been part of it.

'He seems content,' she said, tucking Jamie's hands back under the blanket.

'He's a very happy baby, most of the time.' Liam flipped the bacon onto slices of bread already laid out on plates on the counter. 'Surprisingly.'

'Why surprising?' They'd taken good care of him so far. Why wouldn't he be happy?

Liam added the second slices of bread to the bacon sandwiches and handed her a plate. 'Well, considering the first thing that happened to him after his birth was being abandoned...'

'Since he can't focus his eyes properly or control his hands, I doubt that the significance of that event has hit him just yet,' Alice said drily.

'Maybe not. But it's only a matter of time.' Liam took a large bite of his sandwich, as if trying to stop himself talking.

Alice considered him across the table. This wasn't just idle talk. This was personal for him, somehow.

'Who abandoned you?' she asked softly.

Liam took another bite instead of answering.

'Ever since we found him... This is personal for you, isn't it? Because of your dad?'

'My father,' Liam corrected. 'I never knew him well enough to call him Dad.'

'Right.' Alice trawled through her sleep-deprived brain to try to remember what she knew about Liam's family. She knew that his father had never acknowledged that he was his son before he'd died. That had to impact on a person. And his mother... What had happened to his mother? 'What about your mum?'

'She died when I was ten.'

'Oh. I'm sorry.' Death wasn't abandonment, she knew, but it could feel like it. She frowned. 'Where did you go?' He'd mentioned foster parents the night before, but in the middle of everything it hadn't fully registered. And it didn't answer the obvious question: Why hadn't he gone to stay with Rose?

'Does it matter?' he said irritably, his usual cool evaporating for a moment.

'You don't have to—' she started, but he interrupted her with a heavy sigh.

'No. It's fine.' He shrugged. 'It was all a long time ago. I stayed with some of my mum's family for a while, over in Australia. But they couldn't cope with me.'

'You were a troublemaker?'

'I was a nightmare.'

She could imagine it easily enough. A guy didn't get as rich and successful as young as Liam had unless he was willing to take risks. And that kind of risk-taking didn't tend to manifest itself well in teenage boys, from her observations.

'So where did you go then?'

He looked down at Jamie. 'Foster homes, mostly. Like I told you last night. I bounced around between a few of them and the care homes.'

'Why didn't you come to Thornwood? I'm sure Rose would—'

'Yeah, well, maybe you didn't know Rose as well as you think,' he snapped, loud enough to draw a startled cry from Jamie.

Alice dropped her sandwich to her plate and went to pick the baby up, glad of the excuse to turn her back on Liam's anger. Even if it wasn't really directed at her, just the sound of it made her nervous, and she didn't need him seeing that.

Behind her, he sighed, loud enough for her to hear. 'Sorry. I didn't mean to upset Jamie.'

'He's fine.' And he was. Alice held him close against her body and remembered how special it had felt, every time he'd woken up in the night wanting her. She was sure it was the sort of feeling that wore off as the sleep deprivation increased, but for now it was magical. Especially since she wouldn't be doing it for long.

Sucking in a breath, she turned back to face him. 'What happened with Rose?'

CHAPTER NINE

LIAM TIPPED HIS chair back on two legs and stared at his hands. What had happened with Rose? That was a question he'd asked himself a million times over the years. What had he done at ten years old that meant he wasn't good enough for his great-aunt? And what had changed between then and now, to mean that she'd left him everything she held dear?

Looking up, he met Alice's eyes. She'd known Rose better than anyone at the end, he'd bet. Maybe she'd be able to explain it to him.

'I was ten,' he said, figuring it was easiest to just get it over with. She'd find out eventually. It might as well be him that told her. 'I'd been kicked out of my uncle's house in Brisbane, and the authorities were running out of places to put me. Someone figured out about my father's family over here in the UK and got in touch with Rose, who was more or less all that was left of it by then. She agreed to meet me.'

'You came to Thornwood?'

'Briefly.' Sighing, he let his chair drop back to all four legs again. 'I pitched up here, freezing cold and miserable, and this creepy old guy answered the door—the butler. He looked down his long nose at me and... I knew this wasn't the place for me.'

'What did you do?' From her tone, Liam knew she'd probably already guessed. Apparently he was getting predictable in his old age.

'I acted up. I was rude, objectionable and did everything I could to make sure Rose wouldn't take me in.'

'And she didn't.'

'No, she didn't.' What he didn't tell her, of course, was how much he'd wanted her to. How desperate he'd been for someone—even this old lady who was his only link to his father—to look past his act and see how much he needed her.

Of course, she hadn't.

'She sent you back?'

'Worse.' Liam tried to stop the pain in his chest at the memory. 'She looked down into my eyes, stared for a while, then stepped back and said, "Well, he's a Howlett all right. Can't mistake those eyes." That was the first time anyone from my father's family had ever officially acknowledged me.'

'What was so bad about that?'

'Because that got my hopes up.' Just remembering that hope, that brief shining moment when he'd imagined the possibility of family again, made acid burn in his throat even now. He shrugged the memory away. He didn't need that any more. 'But the next day I got the message—she couldn't take me in. So it was back to the foster system for me. It taught me a valuable lesson at least, I suppose.'

'What lesson?'

'That you can't rely on anyone—especially not family.'

He'd expected her to do as all his ex-girlfriends had when he'd expressed the sentiment—tell him he was a cynic, or try to convince him that he just hadn't met the right person yet. But instead Alice gave him a small smile and said, 'It took me twenty-four years to learn that one.'

'A man?'

'Yes.' One of the tiny pieces that made up the puzzle of Alice Walters fell into place. He wanted to know more, but before he could formulate the right question she said, 'That wasn't the last time you saw Rose, though, was it? You said it had been fifteen years…'

Of course she remembered that. Liam sighed. 'She asked to meet with me in London, when I was working on a project there. Turned out she'd followed my progress, my life, from a distance.'

'What did she want?' Alice asked, eyes wide. She was probably hoping for more signs of the Rose she'd known, he imagined.

'First, she wanted to offer me money,' Liam said.

'Nothing so bad about that.'

'And then she wanted me to sign away any claim to Thornwood, or the family title.' He could still feel the rage she'd awakened now. Sitting having polite conversation, sipping tea at the Ritz, and wanting nothing more than to tear down all that civility and history and privilege.

That he hadn't was a testament to the self-restraint he'd learned over the years. He made himself calm, relaxed, because he knew otherwise he'd hit out, hit back, cause trouble. And he wasn't that boy any more.

'What did you say?' Alice asked, her face troubled.

'I told her I didn't need her money, and I sure as hell didn't want her castle or her fancy title. And then I walked out.' And straight into the nearest pub.

Alice frowned. 'But I don't get it. Why did she leave you Thornwood in the end, then?'

'Because her other great-nephew—the legitimate one—died in a car accident seven years later.' Rose wasn't the only one who could keep track of family. 'Bet she was glad I hadn't taken her money then, when I was the only one left.'

'I think she changed, you know,' Alice said softly. 'The Rose I knew... I think she regretted the person she'd been in the past. She tried to make amends.'

'By opening Thornwood up to anyone who needed it.'

'By leaving you Thornwood.'

Liam looked away. He didn't want to think about that. Standing up, he began to clear the table. 'Dr Helene will be here soon,' he said. 'Along with an astounding number of random women, I imagine.'

'So we'd better get cleared up and ready for the day,' she agreed, handing him Jamie. 'Come on, then. Let's see how long it takes us to get him dressed today.'

'Well, you all seem to have survived the night well enough.' Was it Alice's imagination, or was Helene smirking as she said that? The last thing she needed was her friend getting any ideas about her and Liam.

'He wasn't too difficult in the night,' Alice said. Liam shot her an incredulous glance. She frowned. What exactly had he been doing with Jamie since he'd taken over, before he'd started breakfast? Whatever it was, it wasn't sleep, not if the bags under his eyes were anything to judge by. 'We took turns looking after him.'

'And you did a great job.' Helene looked up from her examination of Jamie. 'He seems to be thriving.'

'I take it the mother hasn't spontaneously come forward overnight. Any luck tracking her down?' Liam asked Iona, who was making her own notes.

'None yet, I'm afraid.' Iona shook her head sadly.

Helene handed Jamie back to him and began packing up. 'Basically, all the pregnant women who've been through my surgery lately are accounted for; I suspect she's either from out of town or she's been without prenatal care.'

'It's a miracle Jamie's as healthy as he is,' Alice murmured, watching Liam rock him gently.

'Women have been having babies for thousands of years without modern medicine,' Iona pointed out. 'But, yes, we were all lucky that it must have been a straightforward pregnancy and birth.'

'So now what do we do?' Alice asked, trying to ignore the way her heart beat a little faster. Just because they hadn't found Jamie's mother didn't change the fact that eventually he would have to go to a new family. However much she wanted to avoid thinking about that, she couldn't afford to. She had to keep that knowledge front and centre—and keep her heart safe.

'Give me another day or so,' Iona said. 'I want to check in with a few more places—colleagues, refuges. But if we haven't found her by the end of next week...'

'We're going to have to call the police,' Liam finished for her.

'And start putting the proper procedures into motion, before everything gets more difficult over the Christmas holidays,' Iona said.

'So he'll be taken into care.' Was it Alice's imagination, or did Liam hold Jamie a little closer as he said that?

She didn't blame him. Now she knew a little more about his background, and his own experiences of the foster system, she could understand him not wanting to put another child through that. He hadn't spoken explicitly about the foster carers he'd had, but the fact he'd been passed around more than a few families spoke volumes.

Liam had grown up unwanted, without a home. Of course he didn't want that for Jamie.

Alice wondered if he knew that, even if they protected

Jamie from it now, it was perfectly possible to lose a family, a home, a future, as an adult.

She'd been twenty-four before she'd realised how little others valued her as a human being. And twenty-eight before Rose had helped her find that value again.

Now, she knew, she made a difference. She mattered.

Just not in the way she'd always dreamt of. She'd never be a mother.

Except for right now. These brief few days, this Christmas miracle of motherhood. That was all she had.

And she intended to make the most of every second of it.

On cue, Jamie started to fuss.

'Let me take him,' she said, holding out her arms to Liam. 'He can feel your stress levels rising and it's upsetting him.'

Liam raised his eyebrows, but handed the baby over. Heather, meanwhile, scoffed. 'Stress levels? I don't think he has any. Didn't you say he was the most infuriatingly laid-back man you'd ever met?'

Alice blushed as her own words came back to haunt her. She didn't want to explain to Heather that she knew better now—knew *Liam* better. In fact, she was beginning to suspect that his casual, laid-back nature was actually a deliberate shield or disguise against the rest of the world.

If he didn't let on that he cared about anything, then he couldn't be hurt when no one cared about him.

Alice identified with that more than she'd like to admit.

'Well, since you're all busy playing Weirdly Happy Families here, I suppose I'd better get on with running the place for the day,' Heather said with a sigh. 'I assume you have your hands too full to help,' she said to Alice.

'Literally, right now,' Alice admitted. 'But I'll still be around; I can help out when he's napping or whatever.'

Heather snorted. 'Yeah, good luck with that. You focus on what you're doing. I'll take care of everything else.'

'Thank you,' Alice said, and meant it.

Thornwood Castle could manage without her for a couple of days. Right now, Jamie couldn't.

And it felt strangely wonderful to be needed again.

Initially, Alice seemed relieved to say goodbye to Dr Helene, Iona and Heather and retreat to his rooms with Jamie. But as spacious as Rose's suite was for one, for three it grew quite cramped quite quickly—especially when Jamie grew fussy after his feed and wouldn't settle to sleep.

'We should get out of here,' Liam said.

'Sure, where were you thinking?' Alice asked casually. 'Paris or Tokyo?'

'I was thinking a walk. You could show me the estate. I've done some exploring but I've barely scratched the surface of it this week.' Mostly because he'd been going through legal documents and figuring out how to get his castle back without actually being a monster. And getting to know the castle itself, of course. A building of such size could take years to know properly, and longer to find every hidden nook and cranny. 'Besides, I'd like to see it through your eyes.'

'What about Jamie? We still don't have a pram for him, and it's freezing out there.'

Liam glanced out of the window; she was right. Never mind Jamie, the way the frost still sat on the fields around them told him definitively that he wasn't in Oz any more.

'The good doctor left us this.' He reached into the bag Helene had handed him earlier and pulled out a tiny white snowsuit. It had a fluffy lining, integral gloves and feet, and ears on the top of its fur-lined hood. It was almost excruciatingly cute, and Liam was sure that almost every woman he'd ever met would have adored it.

Alice, meanwhile, looked pained at the sight of it. He was never going to understand her.

'Don't suppose she left a pram?' she asked.

'We have the baby carrier Heather found, remember?' The contraption looked like a rucksack that was missing its middle, but the illustration on the box suggested it would sit on his chest, with Jamie tucked against him. 'I'll carry him.'

'Then I guess I'm out of objections,' Alice said.

'Be honest—you were only objecting because it was my suggestion.' What was it about her that meant she just couldn't ever admit he was right, or that an idea he had might be worthwhile?

'Pretty much.' She flashed him a smile, and he forgave her. At least she admitted her prejudices. 'But it would be good to get some fresh air. And it might help Jamie drop off.'

'Exactly. And that almost sounded like you were agreeing with me for a moment there.'

Alice's face turned serious. 'I'll have to watch that. Bad habit to get into.'

It took a few minutes to get the three of them prepared to leave the castle. First, they all needed to get wrapped up warm enough to cope with the British winter. Then Jamie threw up his milk all over Alice's jumper and she had to get changed. But eventually they were ready. Jamie nestled against Liam's chest, his tiny face peeping out from under his hood with ears. Liam appreciated the extra warmth the minute they stepped outside.

'Jesus, this country of yours is cold.'

'It's yours now too, remember,' Alice commented as she strode off towards the fields at the back of the castle.

'So it is.' The thought was an astonishing one. That he belonged here—on this frozen, far-flung island. Not in the heat and the beaches of the country of his birth. The place he'd spent so long looking for home.

Instead, he'd apparently found it in the last place he'd expected.

No. Liam shook his head as he hurried to catch up with Alice. Thornwood Castle would never truly be home. How could it? It was an antiquated folly full of bad memories and family expectations. The castle wasn't home—it was a money-making scheme, at best.

But the land around it... Liam had to admit that the English countryside looked stunning, coated in a layer of frost that sparkled and shone in the winter sunlight. The air was cold but crisp, a sharp bitterness that woke up every cell in his body as he walked out into it. Overhead, the occasional bird chirped out from the bare trees and as they crested a small rise on the well-trodden path the village of Thornwood sprung into sight below them, all honey-coloured stone and the rising spire of the church. Picture perfect.

When he'd arrived, on that grey, rainy day, he'd decided that winter in Britain was unbearable—lifeless and miserable, depressing and dead. It had fitted perfectly with his memories of Rose and Thornwood.

Today, the world looked different. It looked alive— vibrant and full of possibility—from the wisps of smoke from a cottage chimney, to the warmth of Jamie's body tucked against his.

He hadn't expected life from this place. Hadn't for a moment thought he'd find anything that could entice him to stay any longer than he had to.

'It's beautiful, isn't it?' Alice said beside him.

'It is.' He glanced down at her, at her shining face, her hair like spun gold in the sunlight, and knew he wasn't just talking about the view. 'I'm starting to think you might not really want to leave.'

She didn't answer, but he didn't need her to. He could see the truth of it on her face.

Alice came alive in this place too. When they'd first met, he'd thought she was just another Thornwood relic—cold and unfeeling, miserable. But over the week or so that he'd been there she'd already shown him so many other parts of herself. Her passion for her mission, her love for the women she helped, and for Thornwood itself. But more than anything, the way she looked at Jamie.

Her face as she held that baby in her arms told him almost everything he needed to know about her.

But only almost.

It told him how brightly she could love, how fiercely. It told him what mattered to her—that every person had a place they could go that was safe, that could be called home.

But it didn't tell him what had caused the sadness behind her eyes as she looked at Jamie. And Liam knew he couldn't leave Thornwood until he'd found the answer to that question.

He blinked as she smiled up at him, and he felt something unfurl in his chest that he'd almost forgotten had ever been there.

He couldn't be falling for Alice Walters. Could he?

CHAPTER TEN

ALICE LOOKED AWAY from Liam's face, uneasy with what she saw there. Or, rather, how his expression made her feel.

He looked like a man who had found the promised land. Who had finally realised how much Thornwood Castle had to give him. He looked as if he'd come back to life—utterly unlike the laid-back, bored and uncaring man who'd arrived a week ago.

This Liam would want to jump into making changes immediately—which meant getting her out of there.

'Come on,' he said. 'Why don't we take a look around at some possible sites for your women? I think there were some barns over to the east of the castle...?'

She nodded. 'Of course.' He was already walking ahead but she didn't try to catch up, following a few steps behind instead, his earlier words echoing in her brain.

'I'm starting to think you might not really want to leave,' he'd said.

But of course he was finding a way to get rid of her anyway.

The truth was, she *wasn't* sure she wanted to leave. But that feeling had nothing to do with the view, or the castle, or even the women she helped there. Well, maybe the women.

But the biggest reason for that feeling was snoozing happily, his little face resting against Liam's chest.

When she'd looked out over the village, she'd had a vision. A daydream, she supposed, but one so vivid it felt as if she could reach out and claim it for her own.

She'd imagined leaving a chocolate box cottage home and taking Jamie down to the village—as a baby, as a toddler, as a boy. Imagined walking down the path to the local school on a summer's morning, or the playground on a Saturday afternoon.

An entire life with Jamie had flashed before her eyes, as impossible as anything she'd ever wanted. As any of the dreams that had been stripped away from her four years ago.

Jamie wasn't her child, and he never would be. Daydreaming about a future with him could only bring her more misery.

And she wasn't even going to admit to herself the other part of that idle daydream—the man walking beside them, laughing and loving them both.

She hadn't seen his face, but even in her vision she'd known exactly who he was. And Liam Jenkins was an even more impossible part of her future than Jamie, for so many reasons.

No, she had to give up these thoughts. And she had to step up their efforts to find Jamie's real mother. If they couldn't find her, then she'd have to give Jamie up at the end of the week anyway, and who knew what would happen to him then? She was under no illusion that the care system in the UK was any better than the one that had let Liam down.

'What do you think?' Liam asked, and Alice realised, belatedly, that they'd reached the first of the barns he was considering as a possible location for her groups.

She blinked and tried to think objectively for an argument that sounded more impressive than *I don't like them.*

'I know they're not in great shape now,' he went on. 'But you have to ignore the state of them. I can fix all that, trust me. It's more about the location, and the possibility.'

'And the planning permission.' She was bursting his bubble, she knew, but she didn't care. She prided herself on being realistic. If Liam was pursuing flights of fancy with her future, she'd have to rein him in.

Just like she had to quash her own daydreams.

She turned and looked back over the path they'd walked, then spun slowly in a circle to take in the full surroundings. The location was what mattered, he'd said. And the location sucked.

'Won't work,' she said bluntly. 'What else have you got?'

'Hang on. I need more than that.' Liam's smile had faded slightly, along with his enthusiasm. '*Why* won't it work?'

'It's too far from the village. There's no easy road access—and that would be a nightmare to try and get permission for. And the path we just took isn't suitable for pushchairs. So, like I said, what else have you got?'

'Reasonable objections,' Liam admitted. 'But I'll find you your perfect location yet. Come on.'

They viewed three more sites before Jamie woke up hungry. Fortunately the last one—not big enough, and too close to the village this time—was a short walk from the Ring O' Bells, which served a tasty steak sandwich and chips and also had good baby facilities.

By the time they were all suitably replenished, the afternoon was wearing on.

'It's getting towards the shortest day,' Alice noted as

she shrugged on her coat again. 'It'll be dark in an hour and a half. We should head back to the castle.'

Liam nodded. 'Okay. There's one more site I wanted to show you, but it's on our way anyway.'

If it was on their way, Alice was pretty sure it wouldn't work as a venue for her women. They needed to be far enough away from the village that they couldn't be observed going in and out—otherwise a lot of them wouldn't come in the first place. Privacy and discretion were important.

But if it was on their way she couldn't reasonably refuse to view it either. She'd promised she'd be open-minded, so she strapped Jamie onto her front this time and trudged after Liam back up the hill towards the castle in the distance.

After about ten minutes, Liam veered off the path, up a small side track through a small copse of trees. 'I think it's up here.'

Curious, Alice followed. She'd never even noticed this path before, let alone taken it.

Ahead of her, Liam came to an abrupt stop. 'Yeah, no. This place is definitely too small, and I can't see me getting permission to expand as much as you'd need. Funny, it looked bigger on the plans.'

Alice frowned, leaning around him to try and get a glimpse of what he was looking at—and felt her heart stutter for a moment.

It was her cottage. The one from her vision on the hill. Oh, it looked different; it was half-falling-down, for a start. But underneath all that—under the overgrown ivy vines and the gaps where roof tiles were missing—it was her cottage.

Her impossible, dream life cottage.

Which was beyond absurd. She wasn't even staying, and if she was she wouldn't have Jamie with her.

She'd have no need for a family cottage like this one.

'No. You're right. Too small.' She turned her back on the cottage, and Liam. 'Let's go.'

Liam stared at the cottage a moment longer, then turned to see Alice already halfway back up the track to the main road. He frowned after her, trying to decipher what he'd heard in her voice as she'd dismissed the cottage as a possibility.

Of course it wasn't suitable—he'd told her that, for once. But there'd been something behind her words—something he hadn't heard at any of the other apparently also unsuitable sites. It had sounded like...longing? Like the way he'd felt sometimes as a child, wishing for something permanent, something real.

Something his.

Did she want the cottage? Or was the cottage just a symbol of all the things she didn't, couldn't or wouldn't let herself have?

He wanted to know,

He caught up with her easily, taking the path at a lazy jog.

'Shame, really. It's a great cottage. It would make someone a lovely family home, don't you think?' The track was too narrow for them to walk side by side so he couldn't see her face, but he was close enough that he could feel her shoulders stiffen at his question.

'It's very pretty,' she admitted without emotion.

'Did you ever want that?' he asked. 'The whole chocolate box cottage thing. Marriage, a family, not living in a creepy old castle.'

'I tried marriage once. It didn't suit.'

The words were throwaway, as if they didn't matter, but they hit Liam in the stomach all the same.

'You were married?' He tried to imagine it, and couldn't. The Alice he knew would never let any man that close.

Which, now he thought about it, was probably *because* of the aforementioned marriage.

Was this the missing piece of the Alice puzzle he'd been looking for? Part of it, maybe. But not all. There was still so much he didn't understand about her. And this admission was the first hint that she might be willing to give him some more clues.

'For a year and a half,' Alice said. 'It was a disaster, it's over, and I don't really like to talk about it.'

Yeah, he wasn't letting her off that easily. 'What happened?'

'Does it matter?'

'It might.' He couldn't say why, but it *did* matter to him. 'Did he cheat?'

'Probably.' She sighed. 'But not that I know of. Look, really, it was a long time ago.'

'You got married young, then?' She didn't answer so, as they turned from the track onto the main path, he nudged her shoulder as he walked beside her. 'It's still a decent walk back to the castle,' he pointed out. 'And I can keep hypothesising the whole way.'

She stalled to a halt. 'Why do you care?'

He shrugged. He didn't really want to analyse his reasons too deeply. He just knew he *did* care. 'We're working together, living together, looking after a child together… and I know next to nothing about you. I told you all about my shining childhood. Now it's your turn. It's only fair.'

She looked away and started walking again. Then she said, 'Fine. I'll give you three questions. What do you want to know?'

Three questions. So like her to put limits on his curiosity, to find a way to make him play by her rules again. He'd just have to choose carefully, then.

'Why did you split up?' That was an obvious one.

'He was abusive, so I left him.' Her words were almost robotic, as if she was distancing herself from the very memory as well as the events.

Liam clenched his jaw, a strange fury burning through him. He'd known, he realised. He'd already known that Alice had suffered—he'd read it in her eyes, in her words, in her very actions. He'd known all along—but it hadn't felt real until now. And the idea of anyone laying their hands on Alice made his fists clench and his mind rage.

'You have two more questions,' Alice pointed out, totally calm, and he realised he had to get a grip on himself.

'He was violent, I assume,' he mused. Keeping it abstract and factual helped. Looking at the particulars—and not the woman involved. Because if he thought too much about that he was going to lose it. 'And no, that's not my second question. How many times? Did you leave the first time he hit you or...' He trailed off, unable to even articulate the idea.

Alice looked away, her arms around Jamie's carrier on her front. 'The first time was just a push.'

'There's no such thing as "just" when it comes to this.' He'd seen it before. One of his mother's boyfriends who had 'just' slapped her, then 'just' pushed her and then she'd 'just' happened to fall down the stairs. The next time he'd 'just' broken her arm.

Liam had wanted to break his face. But he'd been eight years old and puny with it, and there hadn't been a damn thing he could do.

Just like he couldn't change the past for Alice.

'I know that now,' she snapped. 'But back then...'

'You stayed, then.'

'For a while.' She picked up speed as the castle came into sight. 'Look, we're nearly there.'

'I still have one more question.'

'Then ask it fast.' Alice didn't slow down at all. If anything, she walked more quickly.

Only one more question. It had to be a good one, then. And suddenly he knew what it had to be—the question he'd never been able to ask his mother.

'Why did you stay?'

She sighed. 'Because... Because I wanted the future he'd promised me. A family, a home, a place to belong. I'd built all my dreams on that marriage. I couldn't just give it up so easily. And...I honestly believed that I could change enough, be the person he loved enough that he wouldn't react that way again.'

Liam supposed that made a twisted sort of sense, although a future that involved being violently abused or being someone she wasn't didn't sound like much of one to him. And it should never have been up to her to change, to be anything else or less than what she was. The fault was with her husband, not Alice.

He opened his mouth to say as much, but she cut him off. 'And that was your third question, so we're done with this conversation. Understood?'

Liam nodded his agreement, even though he had an inkling they weren't anywhere near done with this topic. She'd answered everything he asked, given him the whole sorry story.

So why did he feel like he'd been asking the wrong questions all along?

It was almost too easy to settle into a routine over the next few days. Alice made sure to put all the focus on Jamie—

and not the exposure of her confessions—and in no time it started to feel as if this was the way things had always been. They still shared Liam's suite of rooms, taking turns between the daybed and the king-size, mostly, while Jamie slumbered in his travel cot. And if there had been one or two nights that had ended with all three of them sprawled out in the king-size, Jamie resting on Liam's chest as he sat up and held him, half-awake, and Alice curled up beside them, well, she wasn't considering them too closely. With a newborn, she'd learned quickly, you did whatever you had to do to make sure everyone got at least *some* sleep. That was all.

Even if it felt alarmingly like a family sometimes.

Keeping Jamie a total secret had proved impossible—the castle walls echoed with the baby's cries often enough that the regulars, at least, had figured out enough of what was going on to need properly filling in. But it was getting closer to Christmas now, and there was so much going on in the village, at the schools and at home, that the population of Thornwood Castle was of a different make up than usual anyway. There were fewer classes or seminars on careers and first aid at the moment, and more fun events for mothers to bring their children to after school or on the weekends. Maud was running a few Christmas baking classes that had drawn in a whole new audience too.

In the daytime, Liam kept Jamie with him in his study while she worked around the castle, running seminars or managing the lunch rush. She'd check in often enough to help out with feeding and changing him, but while he was still so small he mostly dozed in the pram Helene had found for him, or kicked on his mat. Once, she'd caught Liam with Jamie in his bouncy chair, practising a presentation as if the baby were an investor he was hoping to impress.

When Liam had calls or meetings, Alice took Jamie with her on her errands around the castle, securely tucked in his sling on her chest. There were always plenty of people around willing to take turns for a cuddle or a bottle when she needed to give something else her full attention and he was fussy. But mostly life in the castle went on contentedly, with only the shadow of the social worker's deadline looming over them to darken their happiness.

Until the day that Liam went out at first light for a day of meetings in the city, and left Alice alone with a screaming Jamie.

'I don't know what's wrong with him,' she fretted to Heather.

'He's a baby.' Heather shrugged. 'Sometimes they just need to cry. They don't have any other way of communicating with you, so they do this.'

'But what's he trying to *say?*' Alice tried rocking him again, but Jamie only wailed harder.

'That,' Heather said wisely, 'is the eternal question. Now, if you'll excuse me, I've got work to do and that racket is affecting my concentration.'

'It's affecting my sanity,' Alice muttered as Heather walked away. But what choice did she have but to listen to it?

The day dragged on unbearably. Alice tried everything—walks, milk, changes of scenery, singing—but nothing helped. Several of the women who stopped by during the day offered to take him for a while, but he only screamed louder in anyone else's arms so Alice always ended up taking him back.

'Is he really sick?' she asked Dr Helene, who'd popped by to run a quick clinic at the castle. She tried to hold one every month, for any women who couldn't or wouldn't visit their local GP. 'I thought he felt warm…'

Helene finished her examination and started dressing a red-faced, wailing Jamie again. Apparently he liked being poked and prodded by the doctor even less than he'd liked everything else today. Alice could feel the tension knots in her shoulders getting tighter with every second she waited for the doctor's answer.

'He's got a slight temperature, but that's all. Nothing to worry about,' Helene assured her. 'It's probably a touch of a viral bug—a cold, or what have you. There's not much you can do about it at this age, though. I'm afraid you're just going to have to wait it out.'

'Right.' Alice took Jamie back and tried to hold in a sigh.

'When's Liam due back?' Helene asked. 'I'd stay and help, but I've got more appointments this afternoon...'

Alice shook her head. 'Don't worry. We'll be fine, won't we, Jamie? And Liam said he'd be back this evening.'

What he'd actually said, now Alice thought about it, was that he'd be finished with his meetings by late afternoon, so to call him if she needed him to come back and help then. Otherwise he'd probably grab dinner in town with an old colleague and be back later.

She could call him, she supposed. But she knew she wouldn't.

Calling Liam would be admitting that she couldn't do this. That she wasn't cut out for the job of looking after Jamie. It was one thing to let him do his share when he was at Thornwood. But to call him back from the city because she couldn't cope? Not a chance.

Helene frowned with concern. 'Okay. Well, let the others here help while he's away, okay? Make sure you get some rest. And call me if his temperature goes up any more.'

'I will,' Alice promised. She might not like admitting

she needed help, but if Jamie's health was at risk she'd be on the phone in an instant.

But for now it looked like she should settle in for a very long afternoon with a very sad baby.

Liam tiptoed along the stone corridor outside the suite of rooms he shared with Alice and Jamie. He hadn't meant to be so late home from the city, but dinner had dragged on, and then there'd been problems with the trains... Hopefully, Jamie and Alice would both be asleep by now. Then he could grab a few hours and take over the baby duties from Alice. She must be exhausted, he realised, after a whole day and evening alone with Jamie. He felt more than a little guilty about that—certainly more than he'd expected to. But Alice hadn't called and asked him to come back early, so everything must have gone okay.

He listened against the door, smiling as he heard Alice's sweet voice singing soft lullabies. Maybe not both asleep quite yet, then. Perhaps there'd even be time for Alice to fill him in on Jamie's day—it wasn't as if he was *that* late back, after all.

Jamie let out a long wail, and the singing abruptly stopped. Liam frowned; catching up could wait. First they'd better get their boy to sleep.

Pushing open the door, Liam stepped through, smiling at the picture of Alice and Jamie curled up in the comfy armchair they'd moved up to the suite from one of the sitting rooms. 'Hey,' he said, over the sound of Jamie's cries. 'Everything okay?'

'Just fine. Can't you hear?' Alice snapped, and then she sighed. 'Sorry. He's been like this all day. Helene thinks he picked up a cold or something.'

Liam rushed forward, the need to hold Jamie in his arms, to be sure the little boy was okay, suddenly overwhelming. But as he reached for the baby, he noticed something else—the drying tears on Alice's cheeks, and the raw redness around her eyes.

All day, she'd said. He'd been like this all day. And she'd been alone with him.

And she still hadn't called him back to help.

The realisation stung, but he knew he couldn't deal with that right now. His first priority had to be Jamie—and Alice.

'Go lie down for a bit,' he suggested. 'Or take a bath. Whatever. Let me deal with our boy.'

He could see the exhaustion, relief and pride warring in her eyes, but eventually she nodded. Shifting Jamie into one arm, he held out his other hand to help her up, holding on for a moment too long, trying to convey the reassurance he needed her to feel.

Alice still believed she had to do everything alone. And it was going to be up to him to show her otherwise.

CHAPTER ELEVEN

ALICE STUMBLED THROUGH the bedroom to the en suite bathroom, feeling thoroughly zombie-like. Jamie was still crying but the sound was fainter now, muffled by the doors and walls between them.

Mechanically, she twisted the taps on, waiting for the usual groans and complaints of the plumbing as the water started to flow.

She'd made it. She'd survived a full day on her own with a sick baby. And, she knew, if Liam hadn't made it home when he had she would have survived the night too. Oh, she'd have sobbed, and been exhausted beyond limits she never knew she had, but she would have survived, alone.

Because that was what she did.

But Liam *had* come home. He'd returned and taken over and suddenly it wasn't all on her shoulders any more.

She wasn't alone.

And Alice wasn't entirely sure what to make of that feeling.

She tipped in a good measure of bubbles and climbed in, letting the bathtub fill up as far as it could without overflowing. Bubbles peaked high about the level of the bath, covering every inch of her as she sank into the wonderful warmth of the steamy water.

This was what she needed.

It took her a moment to realise that the crying outside hadn't just faded—it had stopped. Either Liam had some sort of magic touch or Jamie had simply exhausted himself completely and passed out asleep. Either way, Alice was grateful.

Until the light knock on the bathroom door startled her anyway.

'Are you decent?' Liam asked softly.

'I'm in the bath.' Alice omitted the 'you idiot', because he *was* still her boss. Then she looked down at herself and realised that there wasn't an inch of her skin showing under all the bubbles. That probably did count as decent, actually.

'I'll keep my eyes closed, then,' Liam said, and turned the handle. Alice sank down a little farther, just in case, but as he felt his way in and around the edge of the small room to perch on the edge of the closed toilet seat, she realised his eyes really were closed.

'Was there something you wanted?' she asked, confused.

Liam paused for a moment. Then he said, 'Why didn't you call me?'

'We were fine.' Alice didn't like to admit how close she'd come to phoning him for help several times through the day. But she'd made it through. She'd proved she didn't need him or anyone else. And that was important.

Even if, in her current exhausted state, she couldn't fully remember why.

'You weren't fine, Alice.' Liam shifted, and she looked away, not even wanting to meet his closed eyes. 'You were in tears. You *coped*, sure. But that's not the same thing.'

'I didn't need your help,' she ground out. Couldn't he see how well she'd done? She'd survived, alone. Surely someone should be cheering her on for that.

'Maybe you did and maybe you didn't,' Liam said. 'But

the point is, you wouldn't even let yourself ask, no matter how bad it had got. Would you?'

Alice lifted her gaze to his face and realised his eyes were no longer closed. He stared down at her, the understanding clear in his eyes. 'No,' she whispered.

'You don't have to wait until you can't cope alone, until things are truly desperate, to ask me for help, Alice.' Liam's voice was soft and warm, and the compassion in his gaze was mesmerising. Alice couldn't look away. 'We're in this together, remember? As long as Jamie is here, he's *our* responsibility, yours and mine. No matter how hard it gets, or how exhausted we both are. Neither one of us is supposed to do it alone. I'm here, and I want to help. So let me. Okay?'

'Okay,' Alice whispered.

Liam smiled. 'Good. Then I'll leave you to your bath. And maybe even nip down to the kitchens and put us together a late night snack. Okay?'

'That sounds good,' Alice admitted, and he nodded and left, closing the door gently behind him.

He'd meant it. He'd really, really meant it. This wasn't a 'Call me if you need me' with an underlying message of 'I really hope you don't, though'.

This was Liam, promising that she could rely on him. That he'd be there, for her and for Jamie, for as long as this strange situation went on.

And the weirdest part of all was she believed him. She *trusted* him, in a way she'd never imagined she'd be able to trust again.

She trusted Liam Jenkins.

Alice stared at the bubbles around her for a moment, then sank her head down under the water. She'd deal with all the emotions and thoughts that brought up when she'd had some sleep. For now, she was just going to enjoy the lifting of her burden, just for a little while.

Two days later, Jamie snoozed peacefully in the sling, his cold all better, as Alice helped Maud to run her Christmas pudding workshop in the Old Kitchen.

'The Christmas puddings we eat today originated in the Victorian period,' Maud said, handing out bowls while Alice passed around the tub full of wooden spoons. 'Before then, it was more of plum pudding, and before that more of a meaty porridge! But today we're going to make a pudding that everyone at your Christmas table will enjoy. Now, to start with, has everybody washed their hands?'

While Maud got everyone sorted with aprons and ingredients, Alice watched from the bench by the fire, rocking back and forth a little to soothe Jamie. When she'd arrived at Thornwood, Maud had been reluctant to let anyone—even Alice—into her kitchen. In fact, she'd resented having any outsiders in Thornwood Castle even more than Rose had. But over the last year and a half she'd watched the work Alice was doing and warmed to the idea. It had been her idea to start the basics cooking courses, ideal for girls going off to university, or starting their own families or setting up home. They'd proved so popular—and Maud's recipes so delicious—that they not only ran the basics course every month but also offered an intermediate one on occasion.

The Christmas pudding day had been Maud's idea too. 'If I'm making one Christmas pudding, we might as well make a dozen,' she'd said, so Heather had made up fliers, Alice had made enough calls to raise the money to hold it, and the course had been fully booked in no time at all.

The group around the large, battered wooden table chattered as they stirred their puddings. Strange to think that just over a week ago she'd sat at that table with Liam and they'd hammered out their deal. Since that first walk with Jamie, when they'd stumbled across the cottage, he'd found two more possible sites. Each time, she'd headed out with trepidation to view them, even though she couldn't put her finger on what was worrying her. That they'd be no good, that they'd never find a perfect location and Liam would just throw them out? Or that they'd be perfect, they'd get things set up and then it would be time for her to leave? Either way, she wouldn't be at Thornwood any more. She wouldn't have Jamie. And she definitely wouldn't have Liam.

She shook her head and hummed a snatch of 'O Little Town of Bethlehem' to Jamie. She couldn't think about that. Jamie wasn't hers; sooner or later he'd be going to his real, forever family. Either his mother would be found and he'd be taken home, or social services would find him a family to love and raise him. One with two parents, and maybe siblings to quarrel and play with.

Alice had done her research. She knew that she—a single woman of soon-to-be no fixed abode—didn't stand a chance at adopting Jamie, even with his mother's note. And while she could admit that having him in her life had made everything brighter, more worthwhile, how could she dream of taking responsibility for a vulnerable child when she didn't even know where she'd be, what she'd be doing next month? When she couldn't offer Jamie the home he deserved?

Liam could, though. He had Thornwood, and money and a future. He could give Jamie anything he wanted—everything that he'd never been given himself. Would he? Because Alice knew for certain that she couldn't stick around and watch that from the sidelines. See Jamie and Liam make their own family—watch Liam find the perfect mother for Jamie, even, perhaps. See the life that Alice could never have playing out in front of her, taunting her.

No. She'd lost everything once before. This time, she knew, she'd make sure to get out before everything she dreamed of was ripped away from her. It was the only way she'd survive a second time.

The door to the Old Kitchen clattered open, just as Jamie stirred and cried out.

'Looks like I timed that to perfection,' Liam commented from the doorway, holding out a bottle ready for him.

Alice forced a smile. 'You did.'

Liam descended the stairs and crossed the room to hand her the bottle, apparently unaware of the way all the other women in the room were whispering about him. Alice knew what they were saying; of course he looked as handsome as always, despite the same lack of sleep that had left her with giant suitcases under her eyes. And yes, it was adorable the way he knew baby Jamie's schedule so well.

But that wasn't all they were saying, she knew. They were speculating. Heather had taken great joy in telling her exactly how many conversations she'd overheard in the past week about whether Liam and Alice were a couple now.

'You told them all the truth, though, right?' Alice had asked. 'Explained that we're just sharing care of Jamie for the time being?'

Heather had just grinned even wider. It looked wrong on her usually sombre face, Alice decided, and told her so. Which only made her laugh.

Alice had given up at that point.

Easing Jamie out of the sling, she handed him to Liam, who settled onto the bench beside her and started feeding him.

'So,' he asked, giving her a friendly smile, 'what exactly are we doing here?'

And wasn't that just the million-dollar question?

Alice stared at him without answering, and Liam found himself reviewing his innocent question in his mind.

What are we doing here?

He'd meant in the kitchen, with all the spicy, fruity scent and the women, of course. But in an instant he saw his mistake. Because neither of them had ever clarified exactly what it was they *were* doing, beyond keeping Jamie healthy and safe. And occasionally having conversations while she was naked and covered in bubbles.

Not that he'd been thinking about what she might look like under those bubbles. Well, not much. Not at the time, anyway.

And since then…better not to think about it, he'd decided.

'I mean here,' Liam clarified, waving a hand to indicate the industrious baking going on around him.

'Oh! Obviously. Um, making Christmas puddings,' Alice explained, a slight pink blush on her pale cheeks.

'Right. Of course.'

He looked away, staring anywhere except at her. Because he knew exactly where her mind had gone—because his had done the same thing too.

It had been over a week now. Eight days since they'd found Jamie and offered to care for him, while the search for his mother went on behind the scenes. Even the social services lady was starting to look at them with that gleam in her eye that told Liam she was getting ideas.

But Alice wasn't, he knew that. She'd been very careful to maintain every boundary they'd put up—bubbles notwithstanding. She might be letting him help out more since that night, but that was all about Jamie. She wasn't letting him in on her feelings, her thoughts. She'd clammed up completely after her confession about her husband's abuse, and nothing he tried seemed to change that. He'd attempted to draw her out further on her marriage, tried to figure out what question he should have asked but hadn't, but she'd stonewalled him, or changed the conversation to Jamie's well-being. Her past relationships were clearly off limits, and the only things she was interested in discussing were Jamie and Thornwood. It was as if she wanted him to believe that she'd arrived here fresh-faced and with no past at all.

It only took one look at her for him to know that wasn't the case.

Oh, it wasn't as if she looked worn out by life, like his mother had at the end. On the contrary, despite the night feeds and the exhaustion of caring for a newborn, Alice looked bright and fresh and happier than she had when he'd arrived. It was almost as if Jamie had woken something within her, something that had brought her back to life.

If he was honest with himself, it was incredibly attractive, that kind of brightness. As if the way she looked at Jamie, the love she showed there, was enough to make him feel a tug on his heart.

He'd considered it, he had to admit.

He hadn't expected to fall for Jamie the way he had; all he'd intended to do was help out a clearly clueless Alice with the childcare, make sure that Jamie got a better start in life than most kids in his situation. He'd known that sooner or later—and probably sooner—Jamie would go back to his mother or be adopted by a real family, so he'd not even worried about becoming attached. If he'd never managed to fall in love with any of his beautiful ex-girlfriends in all the time he'd spent with them, he'd imagined it would take more than a few nights with a squalling newborn to win him over. Same with his foster siblings; he'd liked them well enough, loved one or two of them even, but it had never felt like it did with Jamie.

No, this all-encompassing love that made his heart feel too big for his chest every time he looked down at that tiny, trusting body…this wasn't what he'd expected at all.

And neither was Alice.

At first sight, he'd assumed she was a gold-digger, after Rose's fortune. Then he'd realised she was a do-gooder, and gone out of his way to annoy her. He'd had enough do-gooders try to interfere in his early life, and they'd always ended up making the situation worse, not better. He had no patience for them.

Except Alice was that rarity—someone who actually helped. Who did real good. Who made a difference in people's lives.

And, given the hell she'd been through, the fact she wanted to improve others' lots instead of just her own, well, that made him admire her. Just a bit.

The woman he'd got to know since they'd found Jamie wasn't at all what he'd expected, and he could understand now why Jamie's mother had left him for Alice to find— even if she did know nothing about babies.

Unbidden, an image from the night before rose up in his mind, like a film playing over and over. He'd walked into their rooms late in the evening, ready to help put Jamie to bed, and found Alice already dozing in the armchair, Jamie fast asleep on her chest. Their breathing seemed in perfect sync and they had matching expressions of peace and contentment on their faces. Alice's golden hair shone in the lamplight like a halo, and he'd thought instantly of those paintings on traditional Christmas cards—of angels, and Mary with the baby Jesus.

For a moment his chest had felt about to burst with emotions he'd thought he wasn't capable of feeling any more. And he'd known, without ever consciously deciding, that all of this—Jamie, Thornwood, even Alice—was no longer a reluctant responsibility for him, something he felt he had to do before he could move on.

It was where he wanted to be.

Alice's eyes had opened even as that realisation reverberated through him, and she'd met his gaze and smiled. And he'd been lost.

So yes, he'd definitely thought about Alice that way—more than he'd like to admit. He'd considered the possibility of keeping Jamie for himself and having Alice at his side to help. He knew that if Jamie's mother didn't come forward a new family would have to be found—and why shouldn't it be them? It might take some persuasion, but Jamie's mother had left him to the two of them. That had to count for something.

Except there wasn't really a 'them', was there? He and Alice weren't a couple, and the only thing that linked them was their love for Jamie.

But maybe that was enough?

He'd seen his mother fall for man after man, every time sure that he was the one—only to be let down time and again. From his father, who'd never even acknowledged their existence after discovering she was pregnant, to her last boyfriend, the one who'd led to their midnight flight to a local women's refuge, just before his mum got sick. He had no interest in that sort of love—something he regularly told his casual girlfriends. Company, conversation, sex, they were all good things. But you couldn't put your faith in them for more.

But Alice was different—not because he loved her, but because she wanted what was best for Jamie. She had no interest in love or forever either, not after her experiences. But maybe she'd be open to a deal—to sticking around long enough to persuade the authorities that they were a stable family for Jamie.

Liam didn't need love, marriage and all that. But he did need Jamie to have everything he'd missed out on. And Alice might just be the answer.

He just needed to find the right way to put his proposition to her.

'How do you feel about dinner tonight?' Liam asked, leaning casually back against the stone wall behind them as they watched the pudding-makers stir their mixtures.

Alice blinked. 'I was…definitely planning on eating some?'

'Great. Then it's settled. Who should we ask to babysit?'

Okay, she was definitely missing something here. 'Babysit? What are you talking about?'

He turned to her, the smile on his lips more charming than she'd ever seen from him before. 'You, me, dinner. Somewhere in the village, maybe. What's the name of that nice gastro pub?'

'The Fox and Hare?' Was he seriously suggesting the two of them go out for dinner? Together? Without Jamie?

Like a…date?

No. She was still missing something. There was an ulterior motive at work here; she just had to find it.

'That's the one. I'll call, make a reservation for what? Seven-thirty? I know you country types like to eat early.' He flashed another charming smile, presumably to show he was joking, but Alice didn't trust it one iota.

'I think you'll find that it has more to do with knowing I'll be spending half the night feeding and soothing a crying baby, so like to get to bed early.' Never mind that he took care of the other half. The man seemed to be able to function on no sleep at all, something Alice had never managed.

'Fine, I'll book it for six, then.'

Six. What was happening at six today? Alice frowned as she tried to visualise her diary. She smiled as it came to her.

'No can do,' she said. 'Tonight is the Christingle service at the village church, followed by the tree lighting on the green. I was planning to take Jamie.' By Christmas, Jamie would be with his real family. This might be her only chance to celebrate a little with him, even if he wouldn't have a clue what was going on.

'Even better,' Liam said, unfazed, pulling out his phone. 'We can go as a family. I'll go call the pub now.'

Alice started with a jolt at his words. A family? Was that what they were?

No, Alice knew that much for sure. She'd dreamed of what a family would feel like for too long not to recognise that this was as far away from it as she could imagine.

And she was more certain than ever that Liam was up to something.

Jamie finished his bottle and she took him back from Liam and brought the baby up to her shoulder for winding. 'Guess we'll find out tonight, huh, baby boy?' she whispered as she patted his back gently.

CHAPTER TWELVE

LIAM SAT BESIDE Alice on the uncomfortable church pew, Jamie snoozing in his arms, and tried to figure out how his plan had gone so off-track.

All he'd wanted to do was take Alice out somewhere private, away from the ears of Thornwood Castle's many, many female occupants, and put his suggestion to her— that they fake being a real family for a while so that he could keep Jamie safe at Thornwood. Easy.

Except the entire population of Thornwood village appeared to have turned out for the Christingle service, and every one of them had wanted to welcome him to town on the way in. Add in all the children racing up and down the aisles excited by their oranges with glow sticks in, and the sweets they'd get to chow down on later, and there hadn't been a moment's peace.

And then there was the other surprise.

Liam sneaked a glance beside him again, looking away quickly when Alice met his gaze. The last thing he needed was her thinking he was staring at her.

Except he was. Or he would be, if he wasn't being watched by an entire village.

He'd known objectively that Alice was an attractive woman. She had that willowy body that she hid under baggy jumpers to keep warm in the castle, but he'd imagined it had to be under there somewhere—hell, he'd seen it in that gold dress the night of the fundraiser. It just seemed to him now that he hadn't really been *looking.* And her features had always been pretty, her honey-blonde hair usually knotted up on top of her head and her face make-up free, but still obviously pretty.

He just hadn't ever thought about what she might look like if she made an effort. Not dressed-up-in-a-costume-to-con-money-out-of-people gold dress effort. Just an ordinary, everyday nice outfit and some make-up.

Church, apparently, was worthy of that sort of effort.

It wasn't as if she was even wearing anything fancy. But just the simple grey velvet skirt and black boots teamed with a bright red sweater transformed her body. He could see every curve, every dip, without having to imagine anything at all.

Except, maybe, what her skin felt like under all those layers...

No. He wasn't thinking about that. It didn't matter that her golden hair hung loose around her shoulders in waves, and he could smell the cinnamon shampoo he'd seen in the bathroom they now shared. The bathroom where she'd hidden that body under all those bubbles... No, definitely not thinking about that. And the fact she was wearing a little make-up, and her lips looked redder and more kissable than ever, didn't matter to him at all.

Not one bit.

Probably.

He had to stick to the plan—and that plan did not involve thinking about kissing Alice Walters. It involved a purely business-like arrangement where they took care of a child in need together—and that was more important than any lusty thoughts the evening might have brought out in him.

Liam focused on the service instead. He wasn't a churchgoer—church had never loomed large in his childhood—but apparently Thornwood Castle, and its owner, were patrons of the village church. The impression he'd got from the vicar was that he'd be expected to attend at least occasionally if he lived at Thornwood.

Which he wasn't planning to do, of course.

That was the other discomfiting side of his evening. From the conversations he'd had on arrival at the church, it was obvious that the village had very clear expectations of him. Expectations that he was going to fail, once he started moving on his plans for the future of Thornwood.

The children, all holding their Christingle oranges, paraded around the sides of the church, glow sticks held aloft as the lights went out. The organ started up with one last carol—'Silent Night'—and the whole church rang with song. The music reverberated in his chest and he looked down to see Jamie staring up at him, mesmerised by the sound.

If he adopted Jamie, he'd be heir to Thornwood, Liam realised. No direct bloodline descendant of the Howlett family, but the whole estate would be his, all the same. The castle, the village, the land—all of it in the hands of a boy whose parents weren't just unmarried—they were a mystery.

Liam smiled to himself. That seemed like a very fitting inheritance to pass on.

The music came to an end and, after a moment of silence, the lights of the church flicked back on.

'Come on,' Alice said, jumping to her feet. 'We need to get a move on if we want a good spot to see the tree-lighting from.'

Liam followed her, manoeuvring Jamie back into his snowsuit and tucking him into the pram they'd left at the back of the church. He couldn't imagine that the switching on of a few Christmas tree lights was really that spectacular, but Alice seemed so excited it was almost contagious.

That, or he wanted another look at how magnificent her legs looked in those long, shiny black boots.

Thornwood village green was situated just outside the church, and already it seemed to be full of people. In the centre stood a large pine tree, its base secured in a box made of logs and wrapped around with a bright red ribbon. The tree itself looked bare, though.

To one side of the green, the choir who had sung during the Christingle service filed out and took their places beside the tree. Then a group of schoolchildren, all in uniform under their thick coats, gloves and hats, were ushered into place by their teacher, until they stood neatly in rows in front of the choir.

Alice darted ahead of him and he hurried to keep up with her, pushing the pram through the crowd and hoping people moved out of the way before he crushed their feet. Finally she came to a halt, not too far from the tree and close enough to hear the kids' choir chattering excitedly.

'What's that for?' Liam pointed to an unexpected cherry picker beside the tree.

'How else did you expect them to light the lights?' Alice asked, eyes wide. The excitement sparkling in them made her more beautiful than any make-up or change of clothes had managed. Liam looked away in a hurry. He had a *plan*, damn it.

To be honest, he'd expected the lights to be lit by a remote—some local celebrity pushing a button that made the whole thing light up. Come to think about it, he'd half expected that local celebrity to be him, but no one had asked.

'Ladies, gentlemen, boys and girls!' A woman's voice rang out over the crowd, and Liam hunted to find the speaker. Then he realised her voice was coming from above. Up in the basket of the cherry picker, to be precise, which had now been raised to the same level as the top of the tree. In it stood a woman dressed all in white, with gossamer wings attached to her back and a shiny silver halo hovering somehow above her head.

Liam stared. 'And here I was thinking that you were the only angel of mercy in this village,' he murmured, and Alice's eyes widened even further. He flashed her a quick grin and turned his attention back to the angel.

'If she was a real angel, she'd be flying,' he heard one of the kids nearby mutter.

'But her wings would get tired,' another pointed out pragmatically. 'This is probably easier.'

'It is my great honour to start the Thornwood Christmas celebrations this year by lighting the village Christmas tree,' the angel said, and a cheer went up. 'Now, if you could all help me by counting down...'

'Ten! Nine!' the countdown started. Beside him, Alice reached into the pram and lifted Jamie out, holding him up to see the tree.

'You know he probably can't even see that far yet, right?' Liam asked, in between shouts of numbers.

Alice didn't answer him. She was too busy murmuring in Jamie's ear, holding him tight as the countdown continued.

'Two! One!'

At the top of the tree, the angel reached out and placed a silvery star on the tip and, as she did so, the whole tree burst into rivers of light—tiny sparkles and flashes cascading down the branches. It was, Liam had to admit, wholly magical.

On the ground, the choirs broke into song—the choristers and the children's voices mingling as they sang of peace on earth and other impossible things. And Liam looked around him and realised that this was unlike any Christmas he'd ever experienced or even dreamt of.

Then he turned to Alice, tucking Jamie back into his pram, her golden hair falling in front of her shining pale eyes, and realised it might just be the Christmas he wanted.

'What did you think?' Alice asked Liam, straightening up from the pram. Jamie hadn't seemed particularly thrilled by the whole event, but she hoped that Liam might have found it more affecting. It was her second Christmas at Thornwood, and she remembered how magical she'd found it the first year she'd been there.

She was glad she'd got to share that feeling with Liam and Jamie before she left.

She turned to hear Liam's answer.

'It was beautiful,' he said, but he wasn't looking at the tree.

He was looking at her.

Alice's next words caught in her throat as his gaze fixed on hers. There was something new in those dark blue eyes, something she'd never expected to see. A heat, perhaps. A wanting.

She stepped back but his hand caught hers and tugged her closer. 'This might just be the magic of the moment speaking, or possibly that angel has cast some sort of spell on me—'

'That's fairy, not angel,' Alice interjected, but he ignored her.

'—but I can't not do this. Just once.' And with that he dipped his head, bringing his lips to hers with the same decisiveness she'd come to expect from him in everything.

Except this time it didn't annoy her. It set her whole body alight like the Christmas tree behind her.

For a shining moment Alice forgot that the whole village would be watching, forgot that Liam was still trying to find a way to get her out of Thornwood Castle. Forgot, even, all those incredibly good reasons she had for never getting involved with another man again.

Instead, she let Liam's kiss wash over her like a cascade of stars in the darkness, bringing the night to life around her.

And then he pulled away and reality came crashing down.

She stumbled backwards and this time he let her go. 'We shouldn't have done that.'

'Oh, I don't know,' Liam said, looking far less flustered by the kiss than she felt. 'Seemed like a good idea to me.'

A good idea? It was possibly the worst idea in the history of terrible ideas. She couldn't get involved with the man who basically had the power to throw her out of her home and force her to abandon her vocation. And she really couldn't risk a relationship with the man who was helping her take care of Jamie—if only because when she had to say goodbye to both of them it might break her all over again.

But Liam didn't seem to understand either of those concerns.

'Come on,' he said. 'Let's get to the Fox and Hare before they give our table away to someone else.'

Alice was freaking out.

Oh, she was keeping it very quiet and civilised, but Liam could tell her brain was going crazy with all the reasons why it was a mistake to have dinner with him. Well, and to have kissed him. He imagined that might be preoccupying her a bit too.

A day ago he'd have agreed with most of her arguments,

he decided, as he queued at the bar in the Fox and Hare. Over at their table, Alice was fussing with Jamie and refusing to meet his gaze.

The thing was, a day ago he hadn't had his brainwave. He was known in his company for flashes of genius—for the one second, game-changing idea. He'd thought he'd had one yesterday, when he'd decided to ask Alice about faking a family so he could keep Jamie. But now he realised that was only the start.

He knew, better than anyone, that family could tear you apart, that love counted for nothing when things went wrong. But that was the beauty of it—Alice knew that too and, crucially, they weren't in love. But he'd come to respect and like her over the past couple of weeks—and he hoped she felt the same about him.

And from the way she'd kissed him back...there was no doubt in his mind that the physical attraction was mutual too, no matter how much she might try to deny it.

Which left them with an unprecedented situation in his life. One he intended to take full advantage of.

Liam took the bottle of beer and the wine glass from the bartender in exchange for the payment he handed over and headed back to the table, already running counterarguments through his brain.

Alice immediately started rooting through Jamie's change bag the moment he sat down.

'What're you looking for?' he asked casually.

She stopped fiddling with the bag and sighed. 'Honestly? I have no idea.'

Chuckling, he nudged the wine glass across the table to her. 'Calm down. Have a drink. This is just dinner, remember?'

Alice looked up at that. 'Just dinner? We kissed, Liam. Well, you kissed me.'

'I might have started it, but you have to admit to being an enthusiastic participant.' He could still feel the touch of her lips against his, the fire they'd sent streaming through his veins. That was no ordinary kiss. And it was *definitely* something they should do again.

Alice flushed, her cheeks as red as her sweater. 'Fine. I might have joined in. A bit.'

'A lot.'

'But it was your idea. So you need to tell me exactly what you're expecting from this.' She looked up and met his gaze head-on, her eyes no longer confused or cautious but demanding and stubborn.

And for once Liam felt strangely compelled to tell her everything. To give her the truth.

'What I'm expecting?' Liam shook his head. 'That's the wrong question.'

'Then what's the right one?' Alice asked, frustration leaking out in her voice. The man was beyond infuriating.

'You want to know what I'm proposing.'

'I think I got a pretty good handle on that,' Alice said drily. After all, that kiss had not been subtle, and they'd been pressed very close together. She could well imagine *exactly* what he'd been proposing. Too well, really, since it probably shouldn't happen. Probably.

Liam gave her a lopsided smile. 'You think this is about sex.'

'Isn't it?'

He shook his head. 'It's about Jamie.'

Alice's blood ran cold, and she resisted the impulse to wake Jamie in his pram and hold him close, just to be sure he was still there. 'What do you mean?'

'I mean, Jamie needs a family.'

'Yes, he does.' Oh, she really didn't like the way that

this was going. 'But there's still been no luck tracing his mother. So social services will probably want to take him soon.' Something she was trying very hard not to think about.

'Except Jamie's mother left him for us to care for, right?'

'I'm not sure that note would stand up in court. And we're hardly the ideal carers for him, are we? You're going to be flying back to Australia as soon as you've got things set up here, and I'll be moving on as soon as we find a new location for the groups and we get everything up and running.' Something *else* she'd been avoiding dwelling on.

Somehow, it seemed her whole life had turned around until she was entirely focused on where she was, and not where she could run to next, for the first time since she'd left her marriage behind in a pool of blood.

'What if we didn't?' Liam asked. Alice stared at him and he went on. 'We both know that family and blood and love and all that don't guarantee you a damn thing.'

'Right.' But she wanted it for Jamie, anyway. Wanted his experience to be different to hers, to Liam's.

'We're both too damaged to even try for that fairy tale, I reckon,' he added, looking to her for agreement. She nodded. 'But we could give it to Jamie.'

Her heart stopped. He was offering her exactly what she needed. 'How?'

'By convincing the courts that we are a stable, loving home for him. That together we can raise him as heir to Thornwood.'

'You mean we fake being a couple?'

The look he gave her was heated. 'It doesn't have to be entirely fake.'

Alice bit her lip. 'I don't understand.' His words didn't seem to make any sense in her brain, and she reached for her wine glass. Maybe there'd be some truth in there.

'It's simple. Stay here, with me. In my suite—in my bed—wherever you want. You know what I want.' He smirked, and she felt the heat flooding to her cheeks again as she remembered how clearly she'd felt what he wanted. 'But that side of things is up to you. All I want from you is a promise that you'll stay at Thornwood with me and Jamie until I'm allowed to legally adopt him.'

'Wait. Until *you're* allowed to adopt him?' Of course, it couldn't be that perfect, could it? Sooner or later, he'd push her out.

Liam shrugged. 'Or us. If you decide you want to stay. And I hope you will. But if you do…that's it. You're in it for life. No running away to the next thing the moment you think you've stayed too long.'

'I don't—'

'Don't you?'

Alice looked away. Of course she did. Every time. The one time she'd stayed—in her marriage—she'd had everything ripped away from her. Her love, her future—and any possibility of having children.

'Why?' he asked softly. 'Why run so much?'

Could she tell him?

She'd have to, she realised, if she wanted what he was offering. It might not be love and fairy tales, but it would be a life together. A family. And he might have…expectations. Ones that she could never meet.

It was only fair to tell him *exactly* what he'd be signing up for.

'We'd be a proper family?' she asked, her voice small.

'You, me and Jamie.' Liam nodded, sure and certain. But then his expression changed, and she could actually *see* the moment the other possibilities came to him. 'And maybe more kids one day, if you wanted.'

He wanted. She could tell by the smile on his face. And

that small, wistful smile was exactly why she knew this could never work.

And yet…

She wanted it. So badly. It was everything she'd ever dreamt of—the vision from that day on the hill—everything she'd thought she had to give up for ever.

Alice was a practical woman. She didn't need true love, not the sort that films and books talked about. She needed an everyday affection, fondness from a partner—someone she could work as a team with.

And hadn't Liam shown her he could give her that already?

Over the past two weeks Jamie had fulfilled every dream she had of being a mother, and many she'd never even imagined.

Between the two of them, they could make Alice happier than she'd ever imagined being.

If Liam still wanted to, after he knew the truth.

'That…the more kids thing. That can never happen.' The words came out staccato and sharp, and they felt like glass in her throat as she spoke them.

Liam's eyebrows furrowed. 'You don't want more kids? Really? Because the way you are with Jamie—'

'It doesn't matter what I *want*,' Alice interrupted. 'I can't have them. Ever.'

'Why?' he demanded, obviously confused.

Alice reached for her wine again and took a long gulp. 'You asked me what happened with my husband. And why I run so much. Well, it's the same answer to both.'

'Tell me.' Liam's tone was no longer demanding. Instead, it was entreating. Begging her to trust him enough to bare her soul and tell him everything.

Could she? Alice knew she had to try.

So she took a deep breath and began.

CHAPTER THIRTEEN

LIAM KNEW FROM the moment she opened her mouth that he wouldn't like this story.

He'd thought he needed to know about her past, her secrets—needed to understand what had brought her to Thornwood, and what would make her run again when the time came. But, in truth, they were her secrets and she had every right to keep them. And now it was time to hear them out loud…he'd give anything not to have to listen. For it never to have happened. For Alice's life to have been blissfully happy and untroubled.

Except, if it had been, she wouldn't be there with him and Jamie.

So he listened.

'My husband… I told you he was a violent man. And I hoped he would change, or that I could, and that we could be happy again. You asked me why I stayed, but the better question is…'

'Why did you leave?' Liam whispered when her voice trailed off.

Of course it was. *That* was the question he should have asked on their walk that day. If she'd stayed so long, what had changed to force her to leave?

'I was pregnant,' Alice whispered, so soft that he had to lean across the table to hear her. His heart clenched at the misery in her voice, the lost expression on her face. He reached out and took her hand, and she squeezed it gratefully.

Whatever had happened to her, just remembering it was enough for her to accept his support. That alone told him how bad this was going to be.

'I was six months gone, and those six months had been so different. He'd been supportive and thoughtful—all the things I thought he was when I married him. I was honestly starting to believe that *this* was what we'd needed to make us happy. That the baby would make him a different person—a father, a loving husband.'

She wasn't the first woman to hope that, Liam knew. He suspected his own mother had believed that, once presented with the evidence of a child, his father would have suddenly welcomed them both into his privileged existence.

He hadn't, of course. And he already knew that Alice's husband hadn't changed either.

'One night, just before Christmas, he came home drunk and furious. I didn't understand, because nothing had happened, nothing was different. But whatever it was that had upset him—and I don't think I ever even knew—he blamed me. He yelled, he glared, and he reached out to push my shoulder. I stumbled back and hit the table and I realised, in that split second, that nothing would ever change. That I could not bring up a child in that house. So I grabbed my bag and started shoving things in it.'

'What did he do?' Liam asked quietly, his stomach already sinking at where the story must be going.

'He followed me around the flat as I packed, screaming abuse at me. But I couldn't hear him any more. I was lost in my moment of clarity, knowing that from this moment my life would be different. It would be me and my child against the world, and I would never let anyone make me feel the way my husband had, ever again. I was so fired up with the possibilities in front of me I didn't even consider the problems. Or what he might do to try and make me stay.

'As I walked out the front door of the flat, into the stairwell of the building, I turned to him and I told him I was never coming back. And then I spat in his face.' Alice looked away, her fingers toying with the beer mat on the table before her. Her gaze darted to Jamie, then away, then back again. Liam didn't push her; he just waited silently.

Finally, she spoke again. 'That was what did it, really. His face turned bright red, almost purple. And he grabbed my arm, yanking me around on the landing outside the flat. And then he flung me down the stairs.'

Liam had known what was coming more or less since the story started. But nothing prepared him for the white-hot rage that surged through him as Alice spoke. He knew that violence wouldn't help the situation, or endear him to Alice, but he couldn't help the primal response that rose up inside him.

He supposed the only thing that made him different from Alice's ex-husband was that he conquered it. Swallowed it down and held Alice's hand tighter instead. He needed her to know he was there. That she could trust him, even if she never trusted any other person again.

'I woke up in hospital two days later, on Christmas Eve.' Alice looked up, and Liam lost his fury in the wide, sad pools of her blue eyes. 'I lost the baby, of course. But there were other complications. Along with the broken bones and concussion, they had to operate to save my life as I miscarried. They did their best, of course. But in the end they told me—' She broke off with a sob, her gaze dropping down to the table.

'You could never have children,' Liam finished for her. 'God, Alice, I'm so sorry. I'm so, so sorry.'

So many things that had puzzled him fell into place as she finished her story. Why she'd kept such a distance from babies—but fallen so completely for Jamie. Why she never let herself believe she could have that happy ever after that everyone else seemed to want. Why she always, always ran. Because if she kept moving she could never care enough about anything for it to matter when it was ripped away from her.

It was as if he'd stripped away a suit of armour from her, and when she met his eyes again he could see the whole of her for the first time since they'd met.

He knew who Alice Walters was now. And he only loved her more for it.

No. Not love. That wasn't what she wanted, or what he needed. He admired her. Liked her. Wanted her in his life very badly.

But that wasn't the same thing at all. It couldn't be.

Could it?

Liam shook his head. This wasn't the time to be worrying about such abstract things as love. He needed to focus on what mattered most—convincing Alice to stay at Thornwood and help him give Jamie the life he deserved.

And maybe, just maybe, he and Alice would find the life they dreamt of in the process.

Alice watched the flood of emotions playing over Liam's face, and knew he'd say no now. That she had to leave. That she couldn't give him what he was looking for.

She was damaged goods. Literally.

'I can't imagine how devastated you must have been,' Liam said slowly. 'But I think I understand now. You, I mean. I think I understand you.'

Alice shrugged. Maybe he did. 'So you see why I can't agree to your plan, then?'

'No. That part still baffles me, actually.'

'I can't give you what you want.' Did he really need her to spell this out? 'I can't give you more kids. Jamie would be it. And if we weren't allowed to keep him…' Then she'd lose everything again. Her baby and the man she'd hoped to build her life with. The man she…

No. She couldn't think that.

But she knew the risks. If she stayed with Liam, if they were together…he'd already taught her to trust again. To hope.

What if he taught her how to love once more?

How could she ever recover from that?

'They're going to let us keep him,' Liam said, with far more confidence than she felt. 'They have to. Trust me.'

She wanted to. Oh, how she wanted to. 'But if they don't?'

What if they take him, and I've already fallen in love with you?

'Then we'll deal with that if it happens. But we'll deal with it together. As a team. A family.' Liam's fingers traced up her arm, rubbing her skin reassuringly. 'Just say you'll give us a chance. Me and Jamie. Please.'

She sighed. 'Let me check I've got this straight. We work together to give Jamie a real family. You, me, him. No promises of love, or anything like that. Just a practical arrangement for Jamie.'

'Exactly.' Liam's expression was so earnest, so hopeful. 'I can't promise you love, not now, not after just two weeks. But I can promise I won't do anything to hurt Jamie, or you, ever. And I'll do everything I can to make us all happy. Our little family.'

He was right; it was crazy to worry about love so soon.

And if they were to lose Jamie, it would be soon too. Iona, the social worker, had said the end of this week. That was only a few days away now. She didn't have to worry about losing her heart to Liam in that time. Right?

And she'd already lost it to Jamie. So why not enjoy these last few days as a family, if that was all she ever got?

Alice stared at Liam's face, at the openness there. This was her chance. Could she take it? Could she stay? For Jamie?

Could she take the risk?

She didn't know. She couldn't promise for ever, just like he couldn't promise love.

But she could offer for now.

Leaning across the table, she placed a hand against his cheek and kissed him softly on the lips.

'Is that a yes?' he asked against her mouth.

'It's a yes for now,' she said, unwilling to commit any further. 'Until we know what the social worker says at the end of the week. If she says we have a chance…'

'We'll take it,' Liam said, and kissed her again.

He'd wanted to leave the Fox and Hare right then, and drag Alice home to Thornwood and to bed, but naturally Jamie chose that moment to wake up, ready for his evening bottle.

'We'll get back to this,' he murmured as he broke away to find the milk they'd brought with them. Alice fell back into her chair on the other side of the table, a pensive look on her face.

He hoped to God she didn't start overthinking this now.

Yes, there were issues to be ironed out. And yes, the chances were maybe fifty-fifty that the plan would even work. But one thing Liam knew for certain—Alice wasn't sleeping on the daybed tonight.

Part of it was lust, he admitted. But another part—a bigger part, even—was the story she'd told him. After hearing that, he couldn't bear her to be out of his sight, not even for a moment. He needed her close and safe. Somewhere he could look after her.

Tucked up warm in his arms, for preference.

The waitress brought their food shortly after and they took turns eating, swapping Jamie between them as he fed, was winded, and fussed. It was, Liam decided, by far the weirdest first date he'd ever had—and not just because it had started in a church, hit terrible lows, practically involved a marriage proposal, and still wasn't guaranteed to end with sex. On the other hand, it had sort of been blessed by an angel, so he let himself be a little optimistic about the outcome.

Eventually, Alice finished her wine and they wrapped Jamie back up into his snowsuit, ready for the walk home. Liam knew logically that Thornwood Castle was only a fifteen-minute walk from the village, but somehow tonight it seemed to take for ever. Finally they reached its ancient wooden doors and Alice eased them open carefully, trying not to wake the sleeping baby.

'Bedtime?' Liam asked as he lifted Jamie from the pram and rested him against his shoulder.

Alice bit her lip, making him think thoughts he really shouldn't be thinking while holding a child, and nodded.

Upstairs, they went through Jamie's usual bedtime routine, minus his nightly bath given how much later than usual it was. Finally he was swaddled in his blanket, asleep in his cot. Liam stared down at him and wondered when he'd become the sort of man who could picture himself as a father.

Hell. A father. Him.

He hadn't thought of it like that before, and for a moment every muscle in his body screamed at him to run.

He'd never wanted kids, never imagined being ready to take on the responsibility. He had no male role models— save perfect examples of what not to do.

But maybe that was enough. He reached down to smooth a curl of fluffy baby hair away from Jamie's forehead and smiled to himself.

Maybe knowing what not to do was all that he needed. Just do the opposite of what every man and family member in his life had done to him, and everything any guy had ever done to Alice, and they'd all be fine.

He hoped.

Turning away from the cot, he saw Alice watching him from the bedroom door, her head resting against the wood as she studied him. In the low light, her hair glowed golden and she'd already removed those incredibly sexy boots. But somehow, seeing her in her stockinged feet seemed even sexier. He'd shared this suite with her every night for over a week, but tonight the air felt thicker, more full of promise.

'Shall we go to bed?' Alice asked, her voice low and husky.

Liam smiled. 'Sounds like a plan.'

Yeah. This was all going to work out just fine.

Alice blinked into the darkness as her exhausted body tried to process what she'd heard.

Jamie. Crying. Of course.

She checked the time on her phone—time for his next feed. It didn't matter to him that his pseudo parents had barely drifted off after what Alice had to admit had been some pretty phenomenal lovemaking.

On autopilot, she made up his bottle, shushing and changing him as she waited for it to reach the right temperature. But even the familiar, everyday actions couldn't clear her mind of the memories of the last few hours—of how Liam's body had felt against hers, or the relief that had flooded through her body as he'd taken her.

She hadn't known how much she'd wanted him, needed that, until he'd kissed her that evening. Now she couldn't imagine not having it again.

And, as much as she hated to admit it, she knew it had only been so good because all the secrets were gone. Because she'd told him everything, left her soul bare, and he'd wanted her anyway.

Not just wanted her. He wanted her to *stay*.

He'd called them a family. The one thing she'd never thought she could have again.

She swallowed hard, her eyes wet just at the thought.

'He okay?' Liam slurred from the doorway, his eyes barely open. He had to be every bit as exhausted as her— possibly more, actually—and he'd still dragged himself out of bed to check on them.

'He's fine,' she assured him. 'Go back to bed.'

But Liam shook his head and slumped onto the end of the daybed, watching her as she settled Jamie in her arms ready for his feed.

'You're good with him, you know,' he said as she sat beside him and reached for the bottle.

'I guess it's one of those things learnt best on the job,' she replied.

They sat together in silence for a minute or two, the only noises in the room the ticking clock on the mantel and the gentle snuffling sounds of a feeding baby.

'Are you okay?' Liam asked eventually. 'About tonight, I mean. About us.'

Alice considered, taking stock of her exhausted but oh-so-satisfied body. 'I'm just great,' she assured him with a smile.

Liam let out a long breath. 'Good. I mean, I know you

enjoyed it…' He flashed her a smug grin and she rolled her eyes.

'As much as you did,' she observed.

'God, yes. But anyway, the physical stuff aside. What we're doing here…'

'It's not the normal way to go about things,' she finished for him, and he nodded.

'Exactly. And after everything you told me tonight… I know you know that it…it might not work.'

Alice swallowed again, her throat suddenly thick with emotion. 'I know.' She cradled Jamie closer. How many more times would she get to do this? To hold his body to hers as he fed or slept?

How would her heart survive if she had to give him back? How would Liam's?

She didn't even bother thinking about what would happen to them. The only tie they had was Jamie. If he was taken from them, what would there be left to fight for? Some incredible sex and joint heartbreak? It wasn't enough.

She wasn't fooling herself. This wasn't love. It was lust, maybe, and convenience. But it wasn't a white cottage with roses around the door, and family lunches and bedtime stories with a sleepy little boy.

What she had was a broken man, a broken heart, and the most perfect baby she could imagine. One out of three was plenty for her—as long as she got to keep that all-important one.

'But I promise you I'll fight for him. For us. For our family,' Liam said, his voice so sure and determined she almost cried. 'I'll do everything I can to give us the future we need.'

'I know,' Alice said, her voice breaking.

Liam reached an arm around her shoulder, holding her

head against his upper arm, enfolding them both in his embrace. The three of them. A family.

It was almost too perfect for her to believe in.

'Do you think his mother misses him?' Alice asked, her voice so soft she wasn't sure Liam even heard her.

Until he replied, his voice rough, 'If she does, then she should never have abandoned him in the first place.'

'No. I suppose not.' Jamie had finished feeding and Alice winded him gently against her shoulder before placing him back in his cot and wrapping him up again. 'Come on,' she said. 'Let's get back to bed.'

If all of this could be taken from her again, then she had better enjoy it while she had it.

CHAPTER FOURTEEN

IT WAS NEARLY CHRISTMAS, Liam realised one morning a few days later, as Jamie slumbered in his bouncy chair beside the desk in the room Liam had taken for his office. When he'd arrived, it had barely been December. Now, downstairs there was a horde of children awaiting the arrival of Father Christmas for some sort of festive afternoon tea with presents. Alice had explained it that morning as she'd been dressing, but he'd been rather more interested in the sight of her in her underwear than the topic of conversation.

Alice. She'd sneaked up on him even more than Christmas had.

How had she gone from an irritation to get rid of to someone he couldn't quite bring himself to imagine his days without?

He shook his head and went back to his list of possible sites for Alice's groups and seminars. It was just familiarity, that was all. Familiarity and fantastic sex. Nothing more.

He'd scoured every inch of the Thornwood estate over the past three weeks—sometimes alone, sometimes with Alice, sometimes with another local who wanted to make him understand the history of the place, and often with Jamie strapped to his chest. The lands were vast, with plenty of outbuildings and sites ripe for conversion—and not one of them suitable for Alice's women.

He sighed, thinking again of the cottage he and Alice had found on that first day. It wasn't at all suitable for the seminars and groups that Alice ran—too small, too close to the village, no potential to extend. But for some reason he kept coming back to it. He'd visited it twice more on his excursions, and the last time he'd even snapped some photos. Pulling out his phone, he scrolled through them again, taking in the whitewashed walls, the tiled roof, the broken windows and the curve of the front door. It needed a lot of care and attention if anyone was ever to live there again.

It wasn't at all what he was looking for. But he knew it would make a perfect home for Jamie.

Liam shut down his phone. He couldn't be thinking about such things. Jamie wasn't his yet—and there was a very real chance he'd never be. The social worker was due back this afternoon to discuss options, now it seemed clear that the mother would not be coming forward. Liam was apprehensive and excited all at once.

But if they were allowed to keep Jamie, maybe he *could* stay at Thornwood. It wasn't something he and Alice had discussed—where they'd live long-term. In fact, they hadn't really hammered out any of the details of their arrangement beyond keeping Jamie. Everything else seemed on hold, until they knew that they had a chance to be his parents.

As a result, he'd never seriously considered Thornwood as a for ever option before. But the more time he spent there...

He flicked his phone on to stare at the photo of the cottage again and remembered Alice's face as she'd looked at it. She'd wanted it, he knew, even if she wouldn't admit it to herself. Just like she'd wanted him but hadn't given a single sign until he'd pushed. Just like she wanted Jamie, even though she wouldn't let herself believe it was a possibility.

He'd worked so hard to convince Alice that things could change. That she could trust him with her secrets. That they could be a family—an unconventional one, for sure, but a family. What was one more step?

Thornwood *could* be home, he knew now. If Alice was there with him.

The very thought made him smile. And, as he looked down, he saw that Jamie was awake again, staring up at him with open, trusting eyes.

Closing down his laptop, Liam unfastened the buckles on the bouncy chair and picked Jamie up.

Time to take his son down to meet Father Christmas. And if he was very lucky, perhaps he'd get a chance to make a Christmas wish of his own.

'Don't you want to go and see Father Christmas?' Alice crouched before the little girl hiding in the corner of the main hall behind the Christmas tree. The girl shook her head. 'Why not? Are you scared?'

The girl nodded, making her blonde plaits bob. What was her name? Alice tried to picture her mother and remember what she'd called her. Bethany, she thought.

Alice wanted to tell her that there was nothing to be scared of. That Christmas was the season of goodwill to all men and nothing bad could happen.

But she knew herself how untrue that was.

'What are you scared of, Bethany?' she asked instead.

'I've been a bad girl,' Bethany whispered. 'My stepdad said so. Santa won't come for me this year.'

Alice's heart ached for her. She was so young to already believe that she was beyond redemption. 'Why don't we ask Santa that?' she said. 'Even if he can't come on Christmas Eve, I definitely spotted a present for you in his sack today. Shall we go find out what it is?'

Bethany's face lit up as Alice led her over to the grotto they'd set up beside the main stairs.

'Your child skills have definitely improved since Jamie arrived,' Heather commented from her position as Santa's elf. 'I'm starting to think you might even like the little monsters.'

'Of course I do,' Alice said, but Heather still looked sceptical. She supposed she couldn't blame her. Until Jamie, she'd kept her distance from the children and babies who came to Thornwood Castle, as much as she could. It just hurt too much to see and hold what she could never have. But now she had Jamie it was as if her heart had opened up again, ready to welcome in all the love she'd been holding at bay.

'And it's not just your love of children that seems to have grown.' Heather nodded towards the stairs, where Liam was descending with Jamie in his arms. Alice held her breath until they safely reached the bottom. She'd got over her fear of stairs to some degree, but she'd never be fully comfortable with them again after her accident.

'Now I know you're definitely talking rubbish,' Alice said absently, smiling as Liam held Jamie up to see Father Christmas.

'Am I?' Heather raised an eyebrow. 'Be honest. You're besotted with the pair of them.'

Was she? Maybe. But Alice was enough of a realist to know there was still a chance it wouldn't last—even if the bubble of hope in her chest reminded her how much she wished it could.

Liam turned and spotted her at last, smiling that lazy, slow smile that melted her insides every time.

'In fairness, they both seem pretty besotted with you too,' Heather observed, before wandering off to help with the next child waiting to see the man in red.

Alice stared after her, computing her words. Besotted? That sounded a little too close to another emotion—one she and Liam had been very clear didn't enter into their arrangement. Which was how it had to stay. Wasn't it? She'd promised herself she wouldn't let herself fall in love with Liam. Especially not before they knew if they could keep Jamie, if they were in this for the long haul. Falling in love now would be a disaster.

Because if it was love that was causing this feeling in her chest, then how would she cope if she lost it again?

'Alice?'

At the sound of her name she spun to see Iona, the social worker, Dr Helene and another pale teenager standing behind her. Not just any teenager. Danielle—her missing assistant. And in that moment her bubble of hope burst.

She knew what this meant. There was only ever one way this fairy tale she was living was going to end—and now apparently that ending was here, at Thornwood.

Her legs wobbling, Alice walked forward to join them— even though all she wanted to do was grab Jamie and run far, far away. Somewhere where all the misery to come couldn't touch them.

But there was no place that could save her from this.

'Hello, Danielle,' she said. 'You must be Jamie's mother.'

Liam watched as Father Christmas—the vicar in a fake beard and red suit, apparently—handed out a gift to a small girl in plaits, who held it close to her body as if it was hidden treasure. It was hard not to smile, not to imagine Jamie, a couple of years from now, excited to meet Santa.

He turned to share another smile with Alice, doing refreshment duty over by the Christmas tree, only to find that she'd gone. He scanned the room and finally spotted her in the archway that led through to the library, talking with the social worker and Dr Helene—and someone else. Someone he didn't recognise.

Frowning, he shifted Jamie in his arms and crossed towards them, trying to ignore the heavy, hard feeling growing in his chest.

'Alice?' he asked as he grew nearer. 'Everything okay?'

She spun and looked at him, then at Jamie, her mouth pressed into a tight line and her arms wrapped around her middle. She looked as if her whole world had fallen apart, and any hope that this wasn't what he thought it was faded. He wanted to take her in his arms, to hold her and Jamie close and never let them go.

God, never. Never let *either* of them go.

The realisation of what that meant hit him straight in the chest and he almost stumbled backwards at the impact.

He didn't want Alice to leave. Not because of Jamie, but because *he* needed her in his life.

Because he loved her. Every bit as much as he loved the tiny boy in his arms.

How had he gone from having no family, no love, to feeling as if his heart and his home were overflowing with them?

And how would he cope with losing them?

'Alice…' He started to move towards her—to touch her, to comfort her, anything. But she shook her head.

'I'm sorry. I can't…' And with that, she dashed away, up the stairs, out of his reach.

'Liam?' Dr Helene brought his attention back to the pale, thin teenager standing with the social worker. 'Is there somewhere private we could talk?'

Dazed, Liam nodded. 'The library. I'll…I'll send for some coffee. Or tea.' He was growing more British by the day. Australia might not even *want* him back at this point.

Especially as he suddenly didn't want to go.

He spoke briefly with Heather, who was hovering nearby looking concerned, then led the small group through to the library. The large table in the centre of the room was clear for once, and he moved to take a seat—only to stop when the young girl approached, her gaze fixed on Jamie.

'You're his mother, I take it.' His words came out hard, but Liam didn't care. Yes, she was young—hardly more than a child herself. But she'd left his boy alone when he was only a few hours old. How could he forgive that?

The girl nodded and raised a finger to touch Jamie's face, stopping just a few centimetres away before she pulled back. 'I'm sorry. I—I—'

Tears were streaming down her face, Liam realised. She looked so, so young, so lost, he could almost feel the ice of his anger cracking.

'Liam, this is Danielle,' the social worker said, putting an arm around the girl. 'Danielle, why don't we take a seat and you can explain everything to Mr Jenkins? Just the way you told it to me.'

The girl nodded and let herself be led to a seat. Liam followed suit and prepared to listen. Maybe not to understand, but he could at least hear her out, he supposed.

It was more than Alice had managed.

The thought tore at his heart, but he pushed it aside. He'd deal with Alice after. First, he needed to fix whatever was trying to tear apart his family from the outside.

'Tell me,' he said. And she did.

It took a while, the story punctuated by sobs and outbursts and the tea tray arriving. But it didn't take long for Liam to get the pertinent points.

Danielle was fifteen. She'd been fourteen when she got pregnant at a party. She didn't even know who the father was, let alone how to contact him.

The party had been one month after her mother died, leaving her alone with her uncaring, emotionally abusive father. She'd gone out to try and have fun, to drink away her pain and her grief.

And instead she'd ended up pregnant.

'My mother was a midwife,' Danielle said. 'I'd seen home births before, even helped at one, so I knew what to do. But I was so scared...'

'Why did you leave him here?' Liam asked.

Danielle wiped at her eyes with another tissue. 'My mum...she used to bring me here sometimes, before she got sick. When she died, Alice hired me after school sometimes to help her out. I think she knew I needed the money. So I knew Alice was a good person. I mean, I didn't know her very well, but everyone could see that. I knew my baby would be safe with her.'

'But you didn't know me at all,' Liam pointed out. 'Why put my name on that note too?' Nobody in their right mind would leave him in charge of a child. But Danielle had been desperate. Maybe that was all it was.

She looked up and met his gaze. 'Thornwood Castle is yours. And Mum always said the lord at Thornwood took care of us, down in the village. She used to tell me stories about her grandma and granddad. They worked at the castle, you see. They were butler and housekeeper. When they got married, the old Lady at Thornwood gave them the cottage in the woods, and that's where they lived until they died. I know things are different these days, and I'm not expecting anything from you, I promise. I just... I hoped that you would feel that too. That you'd look after Jamie, and give him the life I couldn't.'

The butler. The same butler who'd looked down on him so many years ago? Maybe. It didn't matter now, Liam realised. None of it did.

Danielle had wanted what was best for her baby, and she'd trusted them to give it to him. It was a stupid, crazy move—one that had to be born out of desperation rather than logic.

And, in the weirdest of ways, she'd been right.

'But now you've come back for him,' Liam replied. That was the part that stung the most.

Danielle shook her head. 'I can't look after him. My dad… I won't bring him up there in that house. I won't let him go through what me and Mum went through.'

'We've found a place for Danielle,' the social worker put in. 'We're working to help her get herself back on her feet, away from her father's influence. But Jamie…'

'He'll go up for adoption,' Liam guessed, and the social worker nodded.

Suddenly, everything was clear. Crystal clarity, with all doubt swept away. No fear, no uncertainty.

Liam knew exactly what he needed to do. It was no longer a pipe dream, a scheme with no plan behind it. It was his future. His and Alice's and Jamie's.

It was meant to be.

'Let me adopt him. I'll make him my heir. Thornwood will be his one day. And he will be my son, I swear to you, in every way that matters. He'll be loved, he'll have a home and he'll have a family.' Everything Liam had never had, he would give to Jamie. And he'd do it with Alice by his side, showing both of them every day just how much he loved and cherished them.

Liam knew it would be the best thing he ever did in this world.

Alice grabbed another handful of clothes from the drawers by the daybed and shoved them into her suitcase. How had so much of her stuff ended up in Liam's room, anyway? This had only ever been temporary, but from her packing it looked as if she'd moved in.

And now she was moving out again. Out of his rooms, out of Thornwood, out of his life. Out of Jamie's life.

It was for the best, she reminded herself. Jamie would be back with his mother, Liam could get on with his plans for Thornwood, and Heather was more than capable of taking over Alice's work. It was time for her to move on, to find a new start somewhere else.

This had only ever been an impossible dream, and she'd known that from the start.

So why did her heart ache so much?

'Alice!' Liam burst into the suite, his eyes alight and his smile broad—until he saw her suitcase. 'What are you doing?'

'Packing.' She didn't look at him. She couldn't.

It was time to move on.

'You're leaving.' It wasn't a question. 'You're running again, aren't you? Even now. Why?'

'Jamie is going back to his mother. You've got your work to get on with. It's time for me to look for something new too.' She kept her voice steady. She was rather proud of that.

'Danielle is giving him up. I've asked to be considered to adopt him, and Danielle has agreed. The social worker thinks we have a strong case. Alice—' He reached out and pulled her clothes from her hands. 'Stop it. I'm telling you it's going to be okay.'

It's going to be okay. It's different this time. It won't happen again.

How many times had she heard those words? How many times had she believed them?

And yes, this was different. And yes, that small bubble of hope was growing again.

But Alice stamped it down. She knew too well how many ways things could go wrong. The only way to avoid being hurt when everything you loved was torn away was by not loving in the first place.

She'd made a mistake with Jamie; she'd got too close, too fast. And she'd run the risk of the same with Liam. But if she left now, right now, she thought she might survive.

If she stayed, if she fell any deeper…she didn't know if she could make it through losing everything a second time.

'You can't know that,' she said softly. 'You can't know it'll be okay.'

'I can promise I'll do everything in my power to make it okay.' Liam held on to her hands and tried to tug her away from the suitcase, but she resisted. She couldn't let him get to her now. She'd made her decision. 'Alice, please. Trust me.'

She shook her head. 'I'm sorry. I have to go.'

'Why?' She didn't answer. 'Because you're a coward? You're too scared to stay? Too scared to be happy for once in your miserable life?'

That was better. Anger she knew how to deal with. Bitterness and frustration were her old friends—and far more familiar to her than love and kindness. And they made it so much easier for her to go.

'So what if I am?' she spat back. 'You've got no idea what you're getting yourself into, have you? So we looked after a baby for a couple of weeks. That's not parenting. That's babysitting. You're signing up for a lifetime job— and you can't build a family or a home just like one of those buildings you design. It's just a fantasy for you—trying to create everything you never had. It's not as simple as all that, Liam.'

'Isn't it? I think you're the one making it hard. You're so scared to trust in something good you're going to throw everything away.'

'I'd rather throw it than have it taken! You say the

mother wants you to have Jamie. What if she changes her mind? What if the courts say no? What if the father comes forward? There are so many things that can go wrong, Liam. And then what will you do?'

'I thought I'd at least still have you,' he said quietly. 'But apparently I was wrong about that.'

'Me? What use would you have for me then?' Because the idea of it being just the two of them, without Jamie there, with no prospect of giving Liam a child of their own... They'd never be able to adopt another child if the state wouldn't even let them have Jamie. So Liam would grow to hate her, she knew. And she couldn't live like that again. Couldn't see hate where she'd once hoped for love.

No, not hoped for. She didn't need love. Love led to disappointment and pain when it was torn away.

Why would she want that?

'What use would I have for you? Alice, I lo—'

'Don't you say it!' She cut him off, her voice shrill. 'Don't you dare say it. We agreed. We don't do that. We're too broken for that.'

'Well, maybe you mended me. You and Jamie. You made me the man I never even hoped I could be. And if we just stick together—'

'No. You want me to believe in the power of home, and family and even love? Well, I can't. That was taken from me four years ago by someone else who said they loved me. And I won't stay here, waiting for the other shoe to drop. Falling deeper into a life that can be ripped away from me at any minute. I won't do it, Liam. Not even for Jamie. Not even for you.'

And with that, she threw her bag over her shoulder and walked out.

She'd burned the last of her bridges with Thornwood. It was time to start over. Again.

CHAPTER FIFTEEN

'YOU LOOK EXHAUSTED,' Heather said, eyeing Liam up and down. 'Do you want me to take Jamie for a bit so you can go lie down?'

Liam shook his head. 'He's no bother. And anyway, I need to work.'

'You've been doing nothing but working and caring for Jamie since—' Heather broke off, but Liam knew what she wasn't saying.

Since Alice left.

Nobody mentioned it around the castle—although he was sure they were gossiping about it in the village. How the lord of the manor had been abandoned, left holding the baby—literally.

It had been a full week since she'd left. Long enough for Liam to be sure she had no intention of coming back.

He knew why she'd run, of course. Understood her fear, her desperate need not to be hurt again. But he'd hoped he'd shown her, in the time they'd spent together with Jamie, that she didn't *have* to be afraid of that any more. That she could trust him—not just with her secrets, her body, or their child—but with her heart.

But apparently her faith in him didn't run as deep as his faith in them, in their little family.

That was her choice. Just because she was too scared

to live, and to love, that didn't mean he had to be. And anyway, he had Jamie to think of. He'd give Jamie the perfect home and family he'd promised, no matter how much work it took.

'There's a lot that needs doing,' he said. 'Plans to be made. Contractors to hire. Planning permission to sort.' A lot of what he wanted to do was just improving what was already standing at Thornwood, but some jobs would take longer, and need official permission before he could begin. Fortunately there was plenty of other stuff to be getting on with.

'It's two days before Christmas,' Heather pointed out. 'Everyone you need to speak to is probably off at their office Christmas do, having sex on a photocopier or whatever people who don't work in castles do.'

He smiled at her. 'Regretting accepting that promotion?' With Alice gone, he'd needed someone to oversee all his new plans, and Heather had been the obvious choice. So far it seemed to be working well. Thornwood Castle was now officially known as Thornwood Haven. There wouldn't be an aristocratic theme park, or go-karting in the woods. And it would never make him any money—but he'd always been good enough at doing that himself anyway.

No, Thornwood Haven would help women and children and families, not just for a while but for good. And that felt right.

'Never.' Heather paused in the doorway. 'You're doing a good thing here, you know. Rose would be proud of you.'

Liam smiled awkwardly as she turned and left. He hadn't done it for Rose. He'd done it for Danielle, and for Jamie. And for Alice.

Even if she wasn't there to see it.

Even if it broke his heart afresh every time he thought of her.

He looked down at Jamie, contentedly watching from his bouncy chair.

'It's just you and me now, kid,' he said. 'So I guess we'd better get on with it.'

Alice looked up as the door to the café she was sitting in opened and jumped to her feet as Helene entered. Christmas music blared out of the speakers and the baristas were all wearing festive headbands and Santa hats.

It was Christmas Eve morning, and Alice had never felt less festive—not since the Christmas she'd spent in hospital.

Hard to imagine it was four years ago today that she'd woken up to learn that her world had changed. And once again she was spending Christmas Eve reflecting on everything she had lost—except the list was even longer this year.

'How are they?' she asked as the doctor approached her table.

Helene gave a low chuckle. 'Not missing them at all, then? Let me grab a coffee and I'll tell you everything.'

Alice dropped back down to her seat, stirring her already cold hot chocolate, and waited. Impatiently.

She'd thought it would be easy to leave everything behind. She'd done it so many times before, after all. What was so different about this time?

Of course, she already knew the answer to that—even if she didn't want to say the words out loud. That would make it real. That would mean she'd walked out on the only life she'd ever wanted.

And she couldn't be that stupid. Could she?

'So, how're things in the big city?' Helene asked, slipping into the seat opposite her. 'Pining for the country yet?'

'Not the country,' Alice muttered. 'Look, just tell me. What's happening back at Thornwood?'

Helene sighed. 'You could come home and find out for yourself, you realise.'

Alice shook her head. 'No, I can't. Trust me. That bridge is well and truly burned.'

'Is it?' Helene raised her eyebrows. 'Seems to me that there are two boys with a row boat that would be more than happy to help you get back across your hypothetical river.'

Her boys. Liam and Jamie. She hadn't even let herself think of them as truly hers until after she'd left. But now that was the only way she could see them. 'How are they?' she asked again.

'They're fine, on the outside,' Helene said. 'I can't speak for their hearts, though. They miss you—anyone can see that. Liam is working a lot on Haven—'

'Haven?' Alice asked, frowning.

'Didn't he talk to you about it?' Helene looked surprised. 'I thought you must have talked him into it. He's turning Thornwood into a proper centre for the women, children and families of the area. He's doing up the place to make it work better—a proper canteen and better facilities in the rooms, that sort of thing. And he's looking at setting up some activities and stuff for summer camps and the like in the grounds.'

He'd said she needed a name for it, for the services and refuge she provided. And now she'd left he'd given it one.

Haven.

It was perfect.

'But not... He's not going to be charging tourists to visit?'

'Apparently not. And he's planning on staying at Thornwood too, it seems. Heather was telling me about all the furniture he's been ordering for Jamie's room.'

Alice stared down at her half-empty mug, trying to process everything she'd heard. Liam was staying. He was building a life, a family at Thornwood, with Jamie. And he was carrying on what she'd started there, helping people.

And he was doing it all without her.

'I should be there,' she whispered.

'Yes, you should,' Helene said bluntly. 'So why aren't you?'

You're a coward, Liam had said. And he'd been right.

If she was honest with herself, she'd known it the moment she'd left. Known how much she was leaving behind, and how much it would hurt. But she'd hoped by enduring that pain now, she could avoid worse pain in the future.

Except there wasn't only pain in the future she was giving up, was there? There were happy moments, and love and family, and everything else she'd ever wanted.

She'd been a coward to run. But how much more of one would she be to stay away?

She was letting her terror of loss rule her life. Letting her past ruin her chance of a happy future.

And if she didn't face up to that fear now, she never would.

But could she really do it?

There was only one way to find out.

'Helene. Can I get a lift?'

'I'm not sure he likes the Santa hat.' Liam eyed Jamie, who stared balefully back at him from Heather's arms. He'd known asking her to watch him for the morning was a mistake.

'It's Christmas Eve, and he looks adorable,' Heather replied. 'Don't deny it.'

'Fine. But he'll have to take it off to get his snowsuit on.'

'You're going out?' Heather asked. 'Where?'

'Just for a walk,' Liam said vaguely. Heather didn't need to know he was taking Jamie on the same walk they'd taken every day since Alice left. This was private—a pilgrimage for him and his boy.

Liam wrestled Jamie into his snowsuit, forcing a knitted hat onto his head in place of the Santa one, and making sure his gloves were firmly in place. Then he tucked him into his pram, blanket on top, and waved goodbye to Heather as they headed out through the front door.

Outside, the air was crisp and cold and Liam breathed in deeply, feeling it chill his lungs. For someone who'd grown up with Christmases on the beach, and Christmas dinner on the barbie, he had to admit an English Christmas was growing on him.

'Come on, then. Let's go.' The quicker they got there, the sooner they'd be back and in the warm again.

Liam pushed the pram along the driveway, towards the main road, frowning when he saw a car approaching. Was that Helene? Wasn't she supposed to be in the city visiting her sister?

Then the passenger door opened and Alice stepped out, wearing the same red coat she'd worn to the tree-lighting ceremony, her golden hair almost translucent in the winter sun.

Liam's heart thudded against his breastbone as she approached, her movements cautious, obviously uncertain about the reception she was likely to get.

She didn't need to worry, he realised suddenly. He'd thought that he'd been abandoned by people he loved too many times before, that anyone who did that to another person wasn't worthy of his time.

But what he realised now was, it didn't matter how far they went. Only that they came back when they were ready.

'You came home,' he said. Because Thornwood *was*

home now, however unlikely that had seemed a mere month ago.

Alice nodded. 'I...I hope so. I figured some stuff out. Will you listen?'

Liam paused. There was so much he wanted to ask, so many questions he'd imagined demanding answers to, if she ever returned. But now, he realised, he had to let Alice talk. Later, he could ask the only question that really mattered any more.

'Why don't you walk with us?' he suggested. 'We talk best when we're walking.'

'Okay. But first, can I...?' She gestured to the pram and, when he nodded, reached in to lift Jamie into her arms, holding him close as she murmured soft words in his ear.

Liam had never doubted Alice's love for Jamie, but seeing it again, so raw and open, he knew that the love she felt for him was for ever.

He just hoped that the fact she'd come back meant that maybe her love for him could be too.

Alice placed Jamie back in the pram and tucked the blanket around him. 'Okay. I'm ready.'

They walked in silence until they reached the road then, as they turned to follow it down towards the village, Alice started to speak.

'When I told you what happened to me... I've never told that story before, you know. Heather doesn't know... Rose didn't know. Nobody.'

'So why did you tell me?' Liam asked.

'Because...you were offering me the life I wanted. One I didn't believe I could have. And I couldn't accept if you didn't know the truth. Didn't understand that I was damaged, that I could never give you what you wanted.' Did she really think of herself that way? Damaged and broken?

'All I wanted was you,' Liam murmured. 'And I never

saw you as damaged. To me, you were strong. Magnificent. You still are.'

She flashed him a small, uncertain smile. 'The thing is, I realised, when I was away, that I wasn't just thinking about what I couldn't give you. I didn't believe I deserved any of this—to be happy, to have love, a child. Not after what happened.'

'You can't believe that what happened to you was your fault.' Liam stared at her, stunned.

Alice shook her head, just slightly. 'I should have left sooner. I shouldn't have provoked him by spitting in his face. I should…' She sighed. 'There are so many things I should have done. But no. I know it was his fault.'

'Good. So why did you run?'

'The Christmas I ended up in hospital…I lost everything. Not just the husband I thought had loved me, or the child I wanted so badly. But my whole future. How could I trust anyone who said they loved me after that? How could I risk having a family of any sort, when I knew how easily it could be snatched away? I was so scared that it would happen again…that's why I kept running. Why I even ran from you and Jamie, when the two of you were the only things I've wanted for so, so long. To be loved by you. To be a family with you. That's…that's the future I never dreamt I could have. And I ran because I was so damn scared of losing it.'

'You realise that makes no sense at all,' Liam said, reaching out to take her hand, holding it with his on the pram handle.

'I know,' Alice sniffed. 'But in my head…it was the only way I had to protect myself. But when I was gone, I realised something else. I wasn't only protecting myself from pain, I was keeping myself from ever being happy again.'

He sighed, wishing he didn't understand so well—but

he did. Wasn't that why he'd planned to leave Thornwood as soon as possible? So that his past couldn't come back and hurt him again?

'I can't lie,' he told her. 'Even though I knew why you'd gone, I hated that Jamie and I weren't enough for you. That you didn't trust me to make it work—even if we weren't allowed to keep Jamie.'

'I couldn't believe that I'd be enough for you,' Alice said, shaking her head. 'And I was so damn scared of falling in love with you...'

'Scared?'

'Terrified,' Alice admitted with a watery laugh. 'I thought I could run and not get hurt. But the two of you were already too deep inside my heart. I already loved you both too much.'

Love. She loved him. Liam had hoped she might, but he'd never imagined she'd come home and say it, just like that.

But she still hadn't said the most important thing, the one thing he really needed to hear.

She still hadn't promised that she'd stay.

'I realised that you were right,' she said after a moment. 'Not just when you said that I could trust you, but that I needed to. Being with you, loving you...that makes me stronger. And running away from it can only make me weaker again.'

They'd reached their turning. Liam paused and turned to look at her. 'So what happens now?' Because that was all that mattered now. The past was gone. All he was interested in was the future. Hopefully, their future.

'I don't want to live in fear any more,' she said, looking up at him with clear, pale eyes. 'I'm done being scared. I can risk any pain, any loss—as long as I get the happiness that comes along the way, and as long as I have you by my side. I'm ready to make my own future—with you and Jamie. If you'll have me.'

Liam smiled as all the pieces fell into place in his heart. 'In that case, we have something to show you.'

Alice followed Liam and Jamie down the track, her heart buoyant and lighter than it had been in years. Jamie was still there—something that had amazed her at first, but she realised now that it shouldn't. Liam was the right parent for him—and maybe she could be too. She wanted to be, and would strive to be. Maybe that was the most anyone could ask.

But what she didn't know was—where were they going? It looked like the same path they'd taken that day when—

Oh.

Alice stumbled to a stop as the cottage came into view—the one from her vision. Her dream of a happy ever after made solid with bricks and mortar. But instead of the overgrown, unloved wreck she remembered, this cottage had clearly been shown a little TLC.

Outside the front door stood a Christmas tree in a pot, strung with tiny white lights that blinked in the afternoon shadows. Over the cottage door hung more lights— brightly coloured lanterns that made the place look warm and welcoming.

Had someone moved in? When? Who?

'Whose home is it?' she asked, not wanting to step closer if they were trespassing. Not daring to speak the hope that was in her heart.

'Ours,' Liam said. 'Yours and mine and Jamie's, if you want it. Because we both love you too. Me especially— more than I ever imagined I could love. And if you can trust me I'll spend every day showing you both just how much. All you have to do is say you'll stay.'

Alice turned to him, the hope inside her overflowing until all the fear that had clung on was washed away. 'For ever?' she asked.

Liam gave her a lopsided smile. 'Longer, if you'd like.'

Wrapping her arms around his neck, Alice reached up and kissed him, long and deep. 'I'm so sorry I ran. I'm so sorry I was scared,' she murmured against his lips.

'All that matters is that you came back,' he replied. 'We missed you so much.'

'I missed you too. My boys.' She glanced down at Jamie, snoozing in his pram. 'And I promise I'll never leave you again.'

'Thank God for that,' Liam said, and kissed her once more. 'Our family isn't complete without you.'

'I couldn't find home anywhere you weren't,' Alice said, filled with the warmth and happiness that came from knowing that she was home at last.

And that none of them would ever be lonely again.

* * * * *

*If you enjoyed this story, check out these
other great reads from Sophie Pembroke*

*PROPOSAL FOR THE WEDDING PLANNER
SLOW DANCE WITH THE BEST MAN
THE UNEXPECTED HOLIDAY GIFT
A PROPOSAL WORTH MILLIONS*

All available now!

MILLS & BOON®
Hardback – November 2017

ROMANCE

The Italian's Christmas Secret	Sharon Kendrick
A Diamond for the Sheikh's Mistress	Abby Green
The Sultan Demands His Heir	Maya Blake
Claiming His Scandalous Love-Child	Julia James
Valdez's Bartered Bride	Rachael Thomas
The Greek's Forbidden Princess	Annie West
Kidnapped for the Tycoon's Baby	Louise Fuller
A Night, A Consequence, A Vow	Angela Bissell
Christmas with Her Millionaire Boss	Barbara Wallace
Snowbound with an Heiress	Jennifer Faye
Newborn Under the Christmas Tree	Sophie Pembroke
His Mistletoe Proposal	Christy McKellen
The Spanish Duke's Holiday Proposal	Robin Gianna
The Rescue Doc's Christmas Miracle	Amalie Berlin
Christmas with Her Daredevil Doc	Kate Hardy
Their Pregnancy Gift	Kate Hardy
A Family Made at Christmas	Scarlet Wilson
Their Mistletoe Baby	Karin Baine
The Texan Takes a Wife	Charlene Sands
Twins for the Billionaire	Sarah M. Anderson

MILLS & BOON®
Large Print – November 2017

ROMANCE

The Pregnant Kavakos Bride	Sharon Kendrick
The Billionaire's Secret Princess	Caitlin Crews
Sicilian's Baby of Shame	Carol Marinelli
The Secret Kept from the Greek	Susan Stephens
A Ring to Secure His Crown	Kim Lawrence
Wedding Night with Her Enemy	Melanie Milburne
Salazar's One-Night Heir	Jennifer Hayward
The Mysterious Italian Houseguest	Scarlet Wilson
Bound to Her Greek Billionaire	Rebecca Winters
Their Baby Surprise	Katrina Cudmore
The Marriage of Inconvenience	Nina Singh

HISTORICAL

Ruined by the Reckless Viscount	Sophia James
Cinderella and the Duke	Janice Preston
A Warriner to Rescue Her	Virginia Heath
Forbidden Night with the Warrior	Michelle Willingham
The Foundling Bride	Helen Dickson

MEDICAL

Mummy, Nurse...Duchess?	Kate Hardy
Falling for the Foster Mum	Karin Baine
The Doctor and the Princess	Scarlet Wilson
Miracle for the Neurosurgeon	Lynne Marshall
English Rose for the Sicilian Doc	Annie Claydon
Engaged to the Doctor Sheikh	Meredith Webber

MILLS & BOON®
Hardback – December 2017

ROMANCE

His Queen by Desert Decree	Lynne Graham
A Christmas Bride for the King	Abby Green
Captive for the Sheikh's Pleasure	Carol Marinelli
Legacy of His Revenge	Cathy Williams
A Night of Royal Consequences	Susan Stephens
Carrying His Scandalous Heir	Julia James
Christmas at the Tycoon's Command	Jennifer Hayward
Innocent in the Billionaire's Bed	Clare Connelly
Snowed in with the Reluctant Tycoon	Nina Singh
The Magnate's Holiday Proposal	Rebecca Winters
The Billionaire's Christmas Baby	Marion Lennox
Christmas Bride for the Boss	Kate Hardy
Christmas with the Best Man	Susan Carlisle
Navy Doc on Her Christmas List	Amy Ruttan
Christmas Bride for the Sheikh	Carol Marinelli
Her Knight Under the Mistletoe	Annie O'Neil
The Nurse's Special Delivery	Louisa George
Her New Year Baby Surprise	Sue MacKay
His Secret Son	Brenda Jackson
Best Man Under the Mistletoe	Jules Bennett

MILLS & BOON®
Large Print – November 2017

ROMANCE

An Heir Made in the Marriage Bed	Anne Mather
The Prince's Stolen Virgin	Maisey Yates
Protecting His Defiant Innocent	Michelle Smart
Pregnant at Acosta's Demand	Maya Blake
The Secret He Must Claim	Chantelle Shaw
Carrying the Spaniard's Child	Jennie Lucas
A Ring for the Greek's Baby	Melanie Milburne
The Runaway Bride and the Billionaire	Kate Hardy
The Boss's Fake Fiancée	Susan Meier
The Millionaire's Redemption	Therese Beharrie
Captivated by the Enigmatic Tycoon	Bella Bucannon

HISTORICAL

Marrying His Cinderella Countess	Louise Allen
A Ring for the Pregnant Debutante	Laura Martin
The Governess Heiress	Elizabeth Beacon
The Warrior's Damsel in Distress	Meriel Fuller
The Knight's Scarred Maiden	Nicole Locke

MEDICAL

Healing the Sheikh's Heart	Annie O'Neil
A Life-Saving Reunion	Alison Roberts
The Surgeon's Cinderella	Susan Carlisle
Saved by Doctor Dreamy	Dianne Drake
Pregnant with the Boss's Baby	Sue MacKay
Reunited with His Runaway Doc	Lucy Clark

MILLS & BOON®

Why shop at millsandboon.co.uk?

Each year, thousands of romance readers find their perfect read at millsandboon.co.uk. That's because we're passionate about bringing you the very best romantic fiction. Here are some of the advantages of shopping at www.millsandboon.co.uk:

* **Get new books first**—you'll be able to buy your favourite books one month before they hit the shops

* **Get exclusive discounts**—you'll also be able to buy our specially created monthly collections, with up to 50% off the RRP

* **Find your favourite authors**—latest news, interviews and new releases for all your favourite authors and series on our website, plus ideas for what to try next

* **Join in**—once you've bought your favourite books, don't forget to register with us to rate, review and join in the discussions

Visit **www.millsandboon.co.uk**
for all this and more today!